MAY YOU

May You

The Walter Swan Prize Anthology

Edited by

SJ BRADLEY

Valley Press

First published in 2018 by Valley Press
Woodend, The Crescent, Scarborough, YO11 2PW
www.valleypressuk.com

ISBN 978-1-912436-07-1
Cat. no. VP0127

A CIP record for this book is available from the British Library.

Cover and text design by Jamie McGarry.

Contents

May You

May you love and be loved
May you find happiness in proportion to the happiness you give
    others
May your world be one of peace through disdaining conflict
May you learn from what you suffer that you can diminish the
    suffering of all you encounter
May your world be one of kindnesses both given and received
With no expectation, ever, of reward
May the world be the better for your having shared in it
May your memory live on for loving and being loved

Walter Swan

Foreword

THE WALTER SWAN Trust is delighted to be supporting the publication of this very special book. It has been a real pleasure to work on this competition with the Northern Short Story Festival and the Leeds Big Bookend Festival (SJ Bradley and Fiona Gell), with the two competition judges (Anna Chilvers and Angela Readman) and with Valley Press.

In 2014 the Walter Swan Trust was established in memory of Walter Swan (1954 – 2014) to encourage and promote new creative writing. Walter Swan was passionate about writing and encouraging others to be creative, which he did throughout his life and particularly through his teaching and directing. For a great deal of his life Walter was a much-loved English and Drama teacher, spending the majority of his spare time acting, directing and writing in various forms. Having been Artistic Director at the Ilkley Playhouse for a number of years, in 2012 he became the first full time Playhouse Manager, a position he held at the time of his death.

Walter wrote a number of short stories himself, as well as a wide variety of poetry, plays and screenplays. He began work on two novels and has three published non-fiction books, and wrote regular articles as a freelance journalist, mostly for the Yorkshire Post. Walter's non-fiction writing was often on the subject of the Yorkshire Dales, a great love of his which developed after he moved to Yorkshire with his family in 1997. Walter was naturally extremely collaborative and often wrote with others; his most recent writing partner was Yvette Huddleston, with whom Walter worked for a number of years.

The common themes throughout Walter's life were kindness, warmth and humour. He was always sociable and had a great talent for friendship. Much of his time was dedicated to others as a family member, friend, teacher and director, and he provided support, encouragement and inspiration in each of these roles. There are many people who remember very fondly his enthusiastic encouragement and support, whether with their own original writing or with their acting. In his role at Ilkley Playhouse and as a teacher, he was able to provide a platform for people to develop and hone their creative skills, providing invaluable guidance and building confidence.

Walter was passionate about creative writing of all genres and, although he was extremely talented in his own right, it is his enthusiasm for the work of others which is the legacy that the Walter Swan Trust now aims to continue. Walter would have loved this book, and everything that The Northern Short Story Festival does in support of creative writing.

More information on the Walter Swan Trust, including details of other charitable activities and associated competitions can be found online at www.walterswantrust.org.uk.

Niccola Swan

Editor's note

I AM VERY proud to present this anthology of new short stories, an anthology which wouldn't have been possible without the generous help of The Walter Swan Trust, Fiona Gell at Leeds Big Bookend, and my own organisation The Northern Short Story Festival. We are also indebted to our brilliant judges, Anna Chilvers, and Angela Readman, without whom this anthology and prize would certainly not have been possible.

This anthology shows the short story form in all its guises. From the wry humour in "Suits" and "The Change", the slipstream surrealism of "She Only Went Out for Milk One Morning and Came Back The Previous Day" to stories of growing up in "Wonderland", and tales of seething resentment ("The Final Delivery"), this is an anthology that shows the enormous range and technique possible within the form. The writers in this anthology have shown enormous skill not only in the range of subjects they choose to tackle: from regret, in "Already Formed", to war in "How To Begin", but also in the structures they use, and in the prose itself.

The short story form is one that is notoriously hard to master, and yet it is a form that endures. Despite its commercial challenges (literary agents often warn aspiring writers, "don't bother writing short story collections – they don't sell,") it is a form that intrigues writers. A puzzle that is almost impossible to solve, yet one that so many writers at all stages are desperate to crack. From Poe to Carver to Davis and now, the actor Tom Hanks, it seems the short story is one literary form that just won't go away.

Yet short stories can prove a thankless task. Hard to master, a struggle to get published, and even to the successful writer, a form that offers little or nothing in the way of fame, and rarely anything in the form of cash prizes or the sort of money from which you can make a living. Learning to write short stories well can be an endurance feat lasting many years, and is something that many short story writers work towards with little fanfare, and usually hardly anything in the way of encouragement – indeed, many of our families and friends may wonder why we bother to do it at all, when we could be doing almost anything else instead, like perhaps writing a best-selling novel about vampires or sex dungeons, or putting up a shelf. However, it is interesting to note that for this contest, a small first-time contest run in the North of England, we received over 300 entries.

Perhaps it is the challenge itself, or perhaps it is the fact that the short story is the only way within which you can express certain ideas. It seems to be a particularly poignant form for expressing grief and regret ("The Memory of the Day", "Timeless"), a wonderful vignette through which to show your reader the passing of time, and changes in relationships ("The Gap Between Us"), or to make quiet revelations ("All Things Bright and Beautiful", "Unsuitable".) These stories, and the ideas they express, simply wouldn't be as effective in any other form.

One of the drivers behind starting the Northern Short Story Festival, now in its third year, was a desire to celebrate the excellence in writing and publishing the short story. There are many superb publishers of the form in the North: Comma, who not only publish the BBC Short Story shortlist every year, but also numerous excellent anthologies and collections; Nightjar Press, who publish short story chapbooks, normally tending to the weird and ghostly; Valley Press, winners of numerous awards; And Other Stories, who publish excellent novellas in translation, and short story collections, and Peepal Tree Press, the largest publisher of Carribbean literature in the world. In addition, we have many wonderful practitioners of the form in the North of England, all of whom I would love to list by name here, but can't, for fear it would take up far too many pages.

I hope you enjoy this wonderful anthology.

SJ Bradley, January 2018

The gap between us

*D*RIFT. THAT'S WHAT people say, don't they, when a relationship breaks down and there is no loud and obvious cause – no domestic abuse, no adultery, no violent sundering of ways. *We just drifted apart.* In my case, though, I know exactly how it started, the drifting, the slow unravelling of intimacy. It was that day in Montolieu, the little town north of Carcassonne, the day of the storm. We went there in mid September one year, both of us wrung out by the fertility treatment that had not worked, wanting only to flop down in the sun, to eat ripe peaches until the juice ran down our fingers. It was David who suggested Montolieu. It was a book town, he said. Really spectacular, two gorges running either side, squeezing it together like a pair of nutcrackers.

It was quieter than we'd expected, the streets almost empty. When we walked out that first evening, we saw that many of the houses were shuttered, some clearly long abandoned. We ate in the little restaurant opposite the church, outside, under plane trees that rustled in the breeze. The leaves were already falling, floating down into the waters of the nearby fountain. The waiters were young – two good-looking boys who spoke English with an American accent. But their smiles could not dispel the air of melancholy, the feeling of a place in decay.

Our first day was long and indolent. We lay in, bought croissants, wandered the back streets. After lunch, we read and dozed. But on the second day we woke to that peculiar stillness that comes before a storm, as if all nature is hunkered down, waiting for the action. It was too cold to swim in the river or sit outside or do any of the things we'd planned. So we walked down to the tourist office and picked up a bunch of leaflets about local attractions – the castle at Saissac, the old town in Carcassonne, medieval half-timbered houses in Sorèze.

And that's how, later that afternoon, we found ourselves driving to the ruined Cistercian Abbaye de Villelongue, meandering through countryside that was at first green and then increasingly desolate. Finally, the road began to climb. Ahead, at the brow of the hill, I glimpsed parked vans, a flash of something orange. We reached the top, the road bent sharply and to our left we saw more vans and a group of men standing around, almost all of them dressed in high visibility waistcoats.

David changed gear. "What's going on?"

"I don't know. Pull over."

So we turned off, pulling up behind a large van with our engine still running. Two or three of the men turned round. There was hostility in the way they looked at us, a kind of 'Who are you and what do you think you're doing here?' antagonism that was palpable, even at that distance, from the safety of our car. One of the men took a step in our direction. He was a large man, his face partially obscured by a blue cap.

"I don't think they want us here…"

The man took another step towards us.

David swung the car into reverse. The wheels spun on gravel as we accelerated away, back onto the road, down the hill, down down down towards the ruined abbey.

David laughed. "What was all that about?"

"I don't know… we clearly weren't welcome."

"Some kind of meeting maybe?"

"What, on the top of a hill, in the middle of nowhere?"

All the way down the hill we speculated idly about what the men were doing. But then the little village of Villelongue came into view.

Our visit did not take long. In fact, I remember very little about the abbey other than the usual cloisters and carved animal grotesques. Afterwards, we took the path we had seen earlier when we parked, signposted to St Martin Le Vieil. We walked in silence, hand in hand, sometimes pausing so that I could pull at blackberries, cramming the fruit into my mouth. The sky was dark now and the stillness, the sense of imminent, violent rupture, was greater than ever. And then we heard it, the noise, a strange muffled wailing.

I tugged at David. "What is it?"

"I don't know. Some kind of machinery maybe."

We walked on, no longer holding hands but still side by side, so close that the raincoats hanging from our waists brushed against one another. The noise grew louder. It swirled around us, rising and falling, a keening or moaning I couldn't decipher.

And then I heard it more clearly. "It's dogs... it's dogs barking."

David paused. He inclined his head. "Yes... yes, you're right."

Again we walked on. But I was uneasy. The barking. There was something about it, something that disturbed me, that sucked at my attention.

"Do you think it's got something to do with those men we saw?"

"Could be."

"Maybe it's a dog fight."

"A dog fight?"

"Yes, don't you remember, the paper?"

At the airport, while waiting for our hire car, we had leafed through a local paper. The story on the front page had been about an illegal dog fight.

"They all had vans... and the way they looked at us. They clearly didn't want us hanging around."

"Possibly."

I glanced sideways and saw that a gap had opened between us, just a small one, the width of a single body.

"We should do something," I said. "Stop it."

"There's nothing we can do."

"We could tell someone," I said. "The police. We should report it to the police."

David sighed. "It's best if we stay out of it. We don't *know* that it's a dog fight."

I wanted us to run back to the car, to accelerate up the hill, to shout at the men until they fell away, until they pulled the dogs apart. I wanted David to say that this was what we should do. But he said nothing. And in his silence, in his lack of encouragement, I felt how my own courage failed.

"What's the number for the emergency services?"

"I don't know."

"How can neither of us know? What if one of us were to have a heart attack?"

He said nothing. The gap between us grew wider. Soon we were three bodies apart.

"Let's go back. I can't enjoy it… not with that horrible sound. "

"OK."

"We could tell someone at the abbey. The woman who sold us the tickets. We could tell her. Then she could phone the police."

"Yes." But he sounded doubtful. All the way back to the car, we drifted further apart until finally, you could have driven a cart between us, a whole cart and horses.

At the car, he hung back.

"Aren't you coming?"

"No. You go. I'll wait here."

So I went on my own. I blurted out the story in a confused jumble of French and English. When I'd finished, the woman smiled. "It is the day of the hunting, Madame. The men, they are hunting."

"Hunting?"

"Yes. It is allowed. Today and also on Sunday. Twice a week they can do it in the summer."

I laughed out loud with relief. Of course! Why hadn't we thought of that? I thanked the woman and hurried out.

David laughed too when I told him. "And to think we were on the point of calling the police."

We, I thought? *We?* But I said nothing.

The storm broke that evening. We drew up chairs facing the windows and sat in silence watching the juddering of the sheet lightning, the sudden flares that lit up the gorge below. There was no rain, not at first. Then we heard it, the first fat few drops. Slowly, steadily, it grew louder, faster, until suddenly it was as if God had ripped a plug from the sky. It fell in grey walls of water then, cascading from the gutters, roaring down the streets.

In the pause between the thunder, David spoke.

"I already knew Dad was beating Mum up. I hadn't just found out."

"What?" But my question was rhetorical. I knew instantly what he was talking about.

At our first meeting, we'd walked across London all night, dodging taxis and tramps, criss-crossing the Thames like we were stitching it together and ourselves with it. And while we walked, we told one another things, things we had never told anyone. I told him the shameful secret of my anorexia, how at the age of fifteen I had almost starved myself to death, how, as a result, I was infertile. David told me his parents were getting divorced. His father had been hitting his mother, he said. Beating her up. He'd just found out. She'd called him in the middle of the night from a women's refuge. He hadn't recognised her voice... had almost put the phone down on her.

There was a roll of thunder and he spoke again, his voice harsh, accusatory. "I'd known since I was eight."

My mind went back to the walk earlier. *There's nothing we can do. It's best if we don't get involved.*

"I woke up one night and heard them. I listened from my room."

I turned away from the window, from the flickering gorge with its Caliban monsters of rock and boulder, its clawlike trees. But even as I took his hand, I could feel how inside, I felt betrayed. That night of walking across London, I told him everything. His honesty – or at least what I thought was his honesty – triggered mine. I told him about the time we had family therapy, all of us sitting round a table like we were having a meal only there was no food, just this horribly sweet hot chocolate in plastic cups. I told him how, as a toddler, I piled books and toys on top of my baby sister, two puzzles on her face, a boxed set of Beatrix Potter on her tummy. With these and other confessions, we wove ourselves together, thread by sticky thread. And now he was snipping at this web. Snip, snip, snip went his scissors!

"So you see I've always been a coward."

"No… no… you were a child."

"Not at sixteen I wasn't. Not at seventeen and eighteen. I could have done something then. I *should* have done something."

I stroked his hand. I drew him towards me and held him close. But already his admission was separating us, pulling us apart in a way neither of us could have foreseen.

That night we slept as we always did, limb-tangled, head to head, toe to toe. But when I woke, I saw we had rolled apart. Now there was space between us, empty white sheet.

And that space, the crack that opened between us on that cold grey afternoon – it grew. It was not a big crack, not then but even so, it was a weakness, a crevice that could widen. And it did. Week by week, month by month, it grew bigger and fatter until one weekend several years later, sitting at the table reading the paper, my face warm in the sun, the taste of marmalade still in my mouth, I looked across at my husband and realised we had drifted apart. There were whole continents between us now, whole continents of thoughts and feelings we could not, would not share. And in that moment, I heard again the barking of dogs and I knew I could trace it back to that afternoon, to the moment we heard that strange muffled wailing. That is where the drifting started, the unravelling of our love. And I found myself wondering if it would have happened, if we would have drifted apart if there had not been that day, the day we imagined a dog fight.

Zita Adamson

The Place of the Middle

MY MOTHER SAYS my sister is a whore. She stands in the doorway, her dark and toughened hand on her heavy hip. She scowls at me, as I make pictures with the dust. My Mother says, things, they have changed. When she looks at me she sighs a curse from the very belly I was born from. I think she knows my future, has heard me whisper secrets to my sister who is not here.

My Father says my sister is a whore. My Father says I am lazy and wayward and he has tried to beat me into dresses so many times that nobody could accuse him of being a bad father. This morning he threatened me with a stick until my mother weeps, screams that I will run away just like my sister did.

His face shrinks, his lips tighten under his moustache, his eyes crease. If men had tears, he would cry. He looks down at me, howling enough for both of us, clutching at my trousers so he cannot strip me and shame me, and he blames the damned revolutionary guerillas for banning alcohol when he is so in need of a drink.

When he is gone I sit on my mother's lap and she scrubs at my tears as if I were a dirty sheet. Still I grip tight of my trousers untrusting in case she coaxes them off me, loves me into a dress and then into a woman before I can follow my sister. But she lets me loose without trying and I sit quietly and help her sew the tiny guerilla dolls that we sell to the tourists in the market. They buy the dolls and take my picture and stroke my plaits and finger my cheeks and think that I want to be like them. I don't. I scowl at them and think bad wishes on them, except the ones who give me sweets. My Mother clicks her tongue at me, pokes at me to smile more. On days when the tourists don't buy much, she says it is my fault. I am a bad daughter and nobody wants to buy off a girl who scowls like a demon and dresses like a boy.

Boys and dogs and soldiers. They are silly and brutish and wild.

The boys have voices that overpopulate our village, fill it up and dry it up and leave me cross, restless. They hunt in packs for frogs or for smaller boys whom they imprison and torture. The small boys they let go but the frogs die. The women, even their mothers, are afraid of them when they are all together.

"Irma!" they call, irritable because dinner is always far off. I walk past, buckled under the weight of wood and their terrorsome stares. "Come here! We will make a woman of you!"

I turn my head but I do not stop walking, wanting much space between us.

"My sister will come shoot you if you touch me!" I hiss, sucking in air through the gap in my teeth.

They are quiet then.

The boys are scared of the guerrillas.

The boys are scared of the guerrillas and the girls are scared of the boys. After our rice and beans we sit in the hut where the foreigners stay to teach us. We draw pictures with the coloured pens and endless paper, and they stick them on the walls, all of them, even the worst pictures by the smallest children, unless we want to take them home to our families who are more discerning. Mostly the children draw pictures of incredible houses, with doors and windows and many bedrooms, but I always paint my sister, with her boots on and a gap between her teeth like me.

"How can you remember what she looks like?" Jesus sneers, too big for his age, ugly like his father. When we were younger we were friends and we smoked tobacco that we stole from his older brothers. I do not answer him but stare him out with the evil eye until he looks away for fear of dreadful accidents. I do not tell him she sends her spirit to me when I am alone by the river and when I sleep, because my sister, she can do anything now she is with the guerrillas, as everybody knows.

"Ssh my wild piglet," she crooned to me some days ago, crosslegged on my hammock whispering so as not to wake my parents. She looks the same, only leaner and with boots, and she has a scar the shape of the river forming on her left arm. When I ask her of it, she shrugs. "It is better than being beaten by a husband." And I stick my tongue out and crinkle up my eyes to show her I agree. I too think marriage would leave a sour taste.

One of the foreigners, moves past Jesus to ask if the picture is of me. I am afraid that he can see through me with his ghost eyes, blue like a river you can see the fish move in, that he will know my secret future and tell my father. But Jesus answers for me, to impress the visitors, as if it were they who were the hope.

"Irma's sister is a guerrilla."

But if the foreigner knew my secret, I too knew one of his. I had stumbled onto him when I was washing clothes by the river. I found the foreigner asleep in the shade, his white hand cradled into his fist, curled in a ball like my baby brother. His cheeks were indented with tears. When I saw him I thought he too is like me. I can never be a woman and he is not a man. Maybe there are many of us like this, halfway inbetween, forging our own path through the jungle. I would have liked to watch him more but my sister had been impatiently calling to me, had some stories to tell and no time for odd foreigners who were weaker than women.

The foreigners left one day, together, orders from someone some-where, humans with flesh not spirits. We sung them a song to say goodbye and I wanted to tell him that I had seen him with tears so we had a secret each and he had no power over me. But I could not speak enough of our shared language and I did not want him to feel shame in front of the village. And so I said nothing and was relieved my father was too proud to talk to him, and they left and I could be safe.

That evening when my parents were at their work, after I had rocked the baby asleep in my arms and laid him down, his eyes closed against our world, I saw my sister's spirit in the doorway.

"Wild piglet," she beseeched, "Walk with me. It's too rainy to settle up in the mountains." Always glad to escape the domestic hearth, I bribed my other sibling into watching over the little one, left my embroidery unfinished beside him and we strolled a safe distance from the village.

We sat together smuggled away at the fast spot in the river you must not bathe in, hidden from prying eyes and suspicious minds by the rich vegetation. Today she is feeling homesick and battle-worn. Her feet, she complains. They never got used to wearing these boots. I stealthily watch them, hungry for boots of my own.

"You!" she raises her hands. "You are always hungry for something!" But she is grinning and full of love and I know she teases me because she misses holding me with her real raw hands.

"I am worried, Irma" and now I know she is because she never uses the name I was given as a baby. "I sometimes wonder... will we ever... in this struggle..."

I shout out "Of course we will win! We have to!" and I clutch at the worn knees of my trousers, some comfort when even my sister has doubts.

We sit together, and I tell her of home a little longer, but she has many things to do back in her body. Our time together is always too brief. When she sinks back into the mountains I stay alone a while, not eager to return to my scolding mother.

Finally homeward I find Jesus in my path, and I brace myself for his noise. But he is delighted to see me, and snatches my hand and pushes a small wrapping into it. Glancing down, expecting to find a dead creature, it is a tobacco pouch.

"I stole it! From the foreigners!" He announces, pleased as a dog that has just dined. I move to scold but I catch his glee and laugh too, amused that we have outdone the grown ups and that Jesus is keen to share with me. We sit down and make cigarettes and smoke until the nausea grows inside us both and we have that to share too. Eventually the growing darkness and fear of my father's rage and my mother's angst concerns me and I haul Jesus to his feet. We do not say it but both realise tomorrow our friendship will be hidden again. I say goodbye to the mountains and head toward one home, away from this other, toward my present and away from my future even as I grow closer.

I walk to face my father, dreaming of boots.

Tabitha Bast

Growth

DEBRAH STARED THE baby down. It was always necessary to spell out her name twice and more. Supposedly stigmata only happened to Catholics. A boy she'd gone to school with had pinched the growth on another's neck and gotten arrested so severe was the result. Whether she stared it down or the baby lost interest can't be known. The pronunciation too: heavy on the second. As a teenager she'd delved into a number of religions but nothing stuck. The sitcom on in the background was older than her. As in: arcing jets of blood sprayed forth. If her brother or the sister-in-law noticed they didn't say. Debrah suffered from private stigmata whereas the baby was desensitive to pain. Her brother and the sister-in-law were discussing a development that might impact on their property. The baby had its own growth on the back of the neck which squeamed her out. At school Debrah was mainly called Debs. She retained a working knowledge of many of the hagiographies. If the development were to go ahead – the sister-in-law was saying – house prices in the area could fall by two per cent. The sitcom wasn't one she'd ever paid attention to but the plot and the lines were familiar. The baby was a drool machine and parts of the carpet were stained with stretched saliva. She hadn't seen the incident but collective accounts concurred. Any conversation about house prices and the like bored her to almost-tears. Which made Debrah quease. Her name didn't even come from anywhere but a mistake. The sitcom was dated and contained language that would never make it through the editorial process now. What mostly put her off Catholicism was the constant need for absolution. She wondered if the baby also had a condition wherein it overproduced drool. Which had literally happened once. Even she'd had trouble pronouncing her name when young and most people added a syllable; a tmesis-like *o*.

Her brother was disinterested in the conversation. The baby had commenced a slow and meandering crawl that might look to an imaginative observer as though it were circling an enemy. As well as was it a thing she could bring up. Her own and personal home was in a complex which itself had devalued the existing built environment. At some point Debrah must have set down on the floor. It was obvious because of familiar intonations in his speech. A year after the incident one girl produced – under exam conditions – a gruesome rendering of the incident for which she was failed and the work in question destroyed. At least two of the actors had died years before. Also a particular timbre to his voice which word she wasn't sure was correct. The stigmata hadn't been diagnosed on any clinical level and were referred to as much because she was afraid of what they really were. The baby was making garbled noises that sometimes sounded like a cackle. The sister-in-law had deliberately never gotten her name right. It was the culmination of a number of incidents in which the boy who did the pinching was teased and abused and generally humiliated in front of his peers. The baby was literally *gaga-gooing* which Debrah thought cliché. Her brother made no attempt to correct his wife re: her name. The vast majority of Catholics she'd met honestly believed in miracles and the transubstantiation deal. It just wasn't his sort of thing. Most everyone sided with the injured boy because his wounds were visible. If Debrah had lived in one of the properties her own home abutted she wouldn't have protested it the way some people had. Her brother assumed a fixed smile she knew well. The first stigma formed at the base of her palm and coincided with the emergence of a ganglion cyst on the topside of her cuff which had the illusion of being connected. She knew that the baby's congenesis meant not *totally* unfeeling. One consequence of the incident was a series of compulsory workshops that incorporated vague admonitions against bullying as well as abstract maxims about respecting each other. They were married gone less than a year but had been together for several more. The baby abandoned its circuit and headed for the door ajar. One objection was that residents were being restricted to a single parking space per household which just wasn't reasonable considering. Which later and on reflection would be likely bad news. This latter extrusion had a darkness approaching black while the former was like a rash that would not be treated with any OTC topical. Debrah had read about a Swedish village where a statistically unusual number of people could also not feel pain. The baby squeezed through the door and crossed the threshold to the hall. She didn't mind her name so much and it was ingrained of course now so whatever. As educational effort it was a failure. Debrah followed on her knees because neither her brother nor the sister-in-law seemed to have noticed. The boy survived: that much she knew. Something that exercised her was when recently moved-in tenants of new developments objected to the noise and presence of long-standing businesses such as bars or restaurants that had made the area desirable to said tenants in the first place. The brother once sprouted an unusually large goitre that had her refusing to be even in the same room as him for the duration of its prominence and notwithstanding pressure from both parents. A line in the sitcom made her puff a laugh which went unheard or ignored. It was kind of a deal breaker if you didn't believe in the biggies. Something about destroying the thing you loved. About a half metre from the baby's behind could be detected wind. The things she referred to as stigmata stung when she caught or rubbed them on a carpet – for example – like now. Her brother had often joked about that time but still she suspected it'd hurt. She referred to the baby as *It* because of the unclear name plus it didn't look like one or the other. Soon after the incident she'd found one of her own: a pimplesque protrusion-like pill on her side and parallel to the umbilicus. It was unclear even to Debrah if her sporadic visits were taken out of duty or if they sprang from a genuine desire to see her brother. Once she'd scratched herself while asleep; the resultant dried blood on her arms and the bedsheets formed a pattern like the dry drool which further added to her aversion. At the time all this occurred there was another growth that would never get the chance to be diagnosed. Which upon and after discovering she became intensely overaware of and took great caution in clothing and unclothing and bathing. The baby's nappy sagged at the back either through being weighted down or else poorly attached but given what she knew of the sister-in-law it was unlikely the latter. The sitcom had finished and the credits were rolling but there was another episode due because that particular channel always doubled up on shows. Sometimes the thing Debrah called stigmata disturbed her so bad she woke up crying. From an early age she believed females had a higher pain threshold than males because they possessed an extra layer of fat. The baby was categorically out of the front room and unquestionably in the hall. Just the sound of the word *goitre* made her stomach contract. Debrah followed crawling and the kid turned Exorcist-like; winked with a palsied eye. Back in the front room her brother was *umming* and *aha-ing* such that Debrah knew he was no longer paying attention. The base of her hand where the thumb began had stopped itching and begun graduating toward a low burn. Over five per cent of the residents of the village had the condition. Which was just a thing she'd been told. The baby began its ascent. Any distractedness might be chalked up to an assumption of both interest and care. An ice-cream van jingled outside. She remained undecided about the sister-in-law. One very common anxiety is that of doing something accidental-yet-unforgivable while a guest in someone's home. In medical-like cases there are often suspected causal factors even if they remain undiagnosed. Actually she was visiting out of duty. The baby showed no interest in the chimes whereas she'd been conditioned to respond at that age. After the incident there was a trend of nipping at a person with a cry of *Molectomy!* For example: breaking an irreplaceable item of immeasurable sentimental value or dropping the hosts' infant son on its head. Post-sitcom a series of adverts were being broadcast with their volume noticeably louder than the entertainment. The baby's entirety was on the first step. By this point her brother would be disinterested to the point of losing the whole thread. From what could be heard the sister-in-law had moved onto the subject of Corporation Tax. Most homes where a very young person is resident have childproof guards in a number of forms. There was maybe a trickle of blood from her wrist as she reached the first step. So he'd have to play catch-up and his brain would be making connections with things said earlier. There were twelve steps to the upper floor which was two below the average. And about which Debrah knew zip. She determined that the dual clacking she'd been only peripherally aware of was the sound of two out-of-sync clocks that were both in the front room. Actually it might even have been only an imagined outlet that sometimes occurred. The baby was either balancing or tottering and she considered the counterweight in the nappy. His wife's lack of exasperation could mean she was totally inured to this or else oblivious. But which clacking had been driving her unconsciously mad. Debrah didn't mind children so much but not this kid. People had laughed about it his whole life but he was far from being the space cadet most took him to be. The baby was gurgling; a vile and bilious noise that could have been a warning. Her brother would be lost as the sister-in-law moved back to parking restrictions. The stigmata might have cleared up without recourse to medicine. Of course she loved him; of course. The baby was approaching a critical angle and nothing could be done. Their parents actually had her brother tested for a number of things regarding his attention span. It happened as she looked down to check her wrist. Most skin conditions are nothing to be worried about although it's always best to be sure. The sound of an eleven month old baby with a shit-filled nappy bouncing head-first down a staircase is as audic and doomful as you'd imagine. The next time she saw her brother would be after all this and before the rest. Fact: time doesn't stop but you do. The sister-in-law didn't go to the funeral. The ice-cream van moved on. The population of the village at the time stood at seven hundred and eighty four. Certainly it hurt but to what extent will be forever unknown. Corporation Tax is that which is levied on company profits and can be a popular conversational topic at the dinner table.

JL Bogenschneider

Suits

IN THE SOMERSET village where I live three cats have gone missing in the past few weeks. Their owners have posted notices on lamp-posts and railings – grumpy cat faces staring out (why do people never have decent photos of their pets when they profess to love them so much?) and somehow a piece ended up in last week's local paper: "Kitty Killer at Large." Talk about jumping to conclusions.

In a small community like this people get very het up very quickly and I gather some have come to the conclusion that the perpetrator is someone local.

I suspect I may be top of list.

I could be wrong, but people have said things like 'someone with a grudge', 'a weirdo', and although I know I'm neither, I can see how some might think it.

"I don't know why you don't make more of an effort to fit in, Caroline," Mummy often said to me. "You're a lovely person really; if you'd just let people get closer…"

It saddens me still that even my own mother never understood me. I've long since accepted that I'm both an outsider and a bit of a recluse and can't recall a time, even at school, when I wasn't. Certainly, the friends I have had have all been city types, people whose lives you can drift in and out of effortlessly, without commitment. Friends should be like cats, companionable when they feel like it, never cloying or needy.

I never expected to end up living in a village. I grew up in London and only came because Mummy and Pa retired here. Oh it's pretty enough but everyone's all a bit too much in each other's pockets if you know what I mean, and despite what you might think from *Midsomer Murders* people aren't whispering about grand passions, but graffiti, dog poo, and inconsiderate parking.

I often visited them over the years but only ever for a weekend. I never would have dreamt of staying longer. But after they died it suited me to stay, just for a while, and now that 'while' has turned into years.

Once Mummy and Pa were gone it was a blessed relief to be left in peace, even though I suppose I did love them. As they approached their ninth decade I'd been bracing myself for the time I'd have to move here and care for them, but in fact they gave me the greatest gift of all by both dying quickly and efficiently within months of each other while still able to care for themselves. Why can't everyone be that considerate?

After they died, feeling unexpectedly rudderless, I resigned from my job at one of the big City banks – just for a break, not really intending to retire. But knowing how badly adapted the old me was to the strictures of village life, I then had to decide whether it was possible to turn myself into someone more appropriate for the community round here. Well, as I suspected, there are only some things you can change. I now dress far less stylishly – I donated all my power suits and stilettos to charity; I've let myself put on a few pounds and rarely wear make-up these days. But I refuse to let my flame-red curls go grey and I still love the colour purple. But those things are insignificant, what matters is that I found you can't change what you feel.

"I don't know why you don't join more things," Mummy often said. "You'll never find a man if you don't."

But I don't want a man – certainly not now, so that's not a problem.

I used to want one, and throughout my life until I came here there was never long when I didn't have one – sometimes several – simultaneously. Not that Mummy and Pa knew that. Those men weren't the type I could ever bring home. Even though most were wholly suitable in terms of looks and manners and education, they weren't the sort who were available at weekends. Had they been, I wouldn't have wasted those hours bringing them to meet my parents.

I suppose I loved those men, some of them, anyway. Certainly I

loved how they looked – all formal and orderly and unapproach-
able in their city suits and ties and fresh-on-every-day, cotton
shirts – and how they smelt, ultra-clean, trailing aftershave. All
of that was an amazing turn-on. Knowing how, if I wanted to, if
I decided to, I could tempt them to a place where they'd tear off
their jackets and ties as if they were burning, discarding trousers
and shirts in a crumpled heap in their desperation to be out of
them. I used to laugh, imagining how at home, with their wives,
they'd turn into different creatures, hanging those suits carefully
in the wardrobe, cladding themselves in leisure wear I never wanted to see. Only with me were they conquistadors.

It was the final suit that did it; he was younger, although not
that young, and at the end of a client party when I'd assumed I'd
made my mark with him and we'd be leaving together, he just
kissed me on the cheek and whispered, "You're too old. Have
some dignity."

Bastard.

I got over it, of course, and these days I rarely think of any of
them. My new love is my garden; it's my little piece of paradise,
entirely private, not overlooked. I take great pride in what I grow
out there, all the plants colour-matched, regimented, pruned and
primped and perfect. I love the sense of control I have over it;
all those little living things responding to how I treat them and
what I want them to do. When I'm out there I feel that my life
is my own to live how I like… but lately, with all the furore over
these damned cats, there's a danger the rest of the world is coming too close.

I should have followed Mummy's advice and made more of an
effort to fit in.

Perhaps one of the reasons the villagers view me with suspicion
is that throughout both Mummy and Pa's services I sat dry-eyed,
seemingly unaffected, possibly a tad bored. But most of the fu-
neral-goers felt like strangers to me – including those who were
part of the family – and even if I had wanted to blub (I didn't) I'd
never let down my guard.

But probably in other ways I should have tried harder.

At Mummy's do at the village hall, five months after Pa's, there were dozens of people clustered like flies over wine and sandwiches. The obligatory conversation was dire, agonising, and after a while I escaped outside to stop myself from screaming. Moments later I was joined by a man – lanky, late forties who, judging by his breath, had started the party quite some time before.

He grinned, revealing gappy, yellow teeth. "Here you are!"

"Hello."

"Graham Pendleton. Caroline, isn't it?"

"Yes."

"Where you from, Caroline? You don't look like you come from round here," he addressed my breasts.

I paused for so long he had to look up. "London. You?"

"Here, in the village. My missus, Susie, does mobile hairdressing, used to do your Mum."

"Oh." I remembered her as being a small, talkative woman, pleasant. How did she tolerate him? His suit was shiny, worn with all the panache of a Guy Fawkes effigy, his tie bore unthinkable stains. Even outdoors I was assaulted by the smell of ancient sweat.

"Take it you're here for a few days?" He didn't wait for my reply. "Perhaps I could come round for a drink one night?"

I leant closer to him and smiled. "What you need to understand, Graham, is that being an atheist I don't believe in hell, but believe me, if I did, it'd have to freeze over before I'd ever let *you* come near."

Now, with the rumour circulating that I might be the despicable cat killer, I've decided I'd better take some defensive action. The last thing I need is a police officer at my door. I've got a plan and head for the village shop, only a few minutes' walk away, to execute it.

Last week when I went there, three women at the counter stopped talking as soon as I arrived and from the way none of them then knew how to resume their conversation, I guessed what they'd been discussing.

"Hello ladies," I trilled, to add to their discomfort.

"Morning," they muttered.

Unsurprisingly, one then said she had to get going while the other two started browsing the shelves with an unnatural intensity.

Bitches.

This time, Elaine, the two-faced, do-gooder who runs the shop, is alone.

"Good morning," I say, treating her to my best full-on smile. "You don't happen to know where the nearest branch of Cats Protection is do you?"

She looks surprised. "Um, not offhand, but I think Louella who helps out here would know. I could ask her if you like."

"Thanks, I'd appreciate it. My poor old cat, Bouncer, is obviously on his way out so I thought if I got a new kitten or at least found out about getting one, it might soften the impact when he does go. I can't imagine a home without a cat – I feel so sorry for those people who've lost theirs. Absolutely tragic."

"Oh. Yes."

My little performance has obviously confused her. To compound it I ask for a bag of cat litter. "Bouncer usually uses the garden, but since all this I don't dare let him out…"

It's hard not to laugh, watching her brain trying to cope.

On the way back I glance again at the posters of the missing cats. Two males: one sleek black with white paws, and the other a fluffy black-and-white. He, like the third, a grey-and-white female, has a white shirtfront chest. Bob, Monty and Fliss: I know them well, having spied them far too frequently in my garden. These pictures are grainy, indistinct; in the flesh they look so bold, so meticulous, so demanding in their suits and boots – just like those men I used to love. Like them, underneath their cool façades they're arrogant, predatory, doing just what they like, disregarding anyone else's feelings.

They deserve what's happened to them.

Once home, I unlatch the side gate and survey the back garden – as much as I can see from the path – reviewing the patches of dug-over soil, muddy now since the rain. All that mess and destruction – what gave them right to stroll in here and do that? Why didn't they know not to challenge me?

Cats are like that, people say.

Men are like that, my city girlfriends used to say, discussing broken hearts and messy affairs.

There's no controlling them.

But I had to do something to make them stop. Surely that's only just?

I unlock the door, push it open, and drop my bags on the kitchen bench. Unable to stay away, I make my way to what used to be Mummy and Pa's dining room, dreading what I know I'll find there. It smells a bit funny these days, but that's hardly surprising.

I push open the door and there they are, the three of them, one perched on the mantel-piece and the other two on the table, staring at me, ears perked up. They've been busy while I've been out, their suits look freshly washed, they've eaten and drunk what I put down for them, and used their litter trays. Whatever I feel about it, they seem to be enjoying it here.

Unlike those men in suits, I can't run away from them. I've created this problem and now I'm going to have to solve it.

What am I going to do with you? I whisper, as they gaze at me, inscrutable.

I think they know the answer; one of them, dammit, starts to purr.

Dianne Bown-Wilson

The Final Delivery

CHUNG SQUATTED ALONE in the back of the flatbed truck. This was the way with Friday deliveries: the apprentice sat in the air-conditioned cab with Yuen the driver, while Chung kept an eye on the load in the back. He'd long ago resigned himself to this arrangement but today Hong Kong's heat and humidity were more oppressive than usual. His torso glistened with sweat and the towel rolled over the waistband of his trousers was sodden. Not a breath of wind fanned his face, despite the swaying motion of the truck. Chung scowled as he wiped his sweating palms down the side of his trousers.

Although they'd worked together for many years, Chung and Yuen weren't friends. Chung sensed his partner, and now their apprentice, despised him. They thought he was a lowborn person, that his love of old furniture was foolish. They saw nothing appealing in the pieces Chung restored. Yuen called them 'fool the *gweilo* furniture' because only foreigners bought second-hand, expensive pieces, instead of the fresh, cheap furniture he made. This was why Chung was never invited to sit in the cab. This was the reason for the scornful looks that passed between Yuen and their apprentice.

Earlier that afternoon, they'd taken a desk Yuen had made to an office in North Point. He'd crowed about its smooth, plastic-coated finish; how it left no whorls or knots for devils to hide in. But to Chung, it was a no-account piece, dull and characterless, with no life or history. It was as different from the antique cabinet that now sat in the back of the truck, as fried rice was from steamed dumplings.

Chung loved his work as a master restorer; loved the steady rhythm of the sander and the smell of shellac and polish. But it was getting harder to find suitable pieces to restore. His boss had found this cabinet – an enormous piece, a head taller than Chung and wider than the span of his arms – on a farm in Gansu Province. It had been used as a chicken coop and was covered in decades of dirt and droppings. Its back had been cracked and splintered; one of its legs was missing. Using all his skill, Chung had crafted a new leg from a piece of walnut, aged to match, and replaced the back panel. Then the sanding and waxing had begun, allowing the cabinet's beauty to shine out.

Eventually, Yuen bumped the vehicle up on to the pavement outside the buyer's compound. While the apprentice lowered the tailgate, Chung paused to slide a caressing hand under the protective blanket before loosening the canvas straps that had held the cabinet in place. Then the three of them carefully manoeuvred it onto a low trolley and pushed it up a ramp and into the lobby. A security guard called the lift.

The problem became obvious as soon as they wheeled the cabinet up to the lift doors. It wouldn't fit. A measuring tape said it should, but the geometry of the confined lift space said otherwise. Even with the cabinet balanced at an angle, the lift doors wouldn't close.

"Only one thing for it," said Chung. This was the last thing he wanted on such a hot and humid day.

The security guard looked on in sympathy as the three men manoeuvred the piece back into the lobby and through the fire exit. They began the long and tortuous job of heaving the cabinet up to the twelfth floor.

They'd done this before, walked pieces too big to fit in a lift up dim stairwells, Chung and the apprentice at the bottom taking the weight, Yuen at the top steering and supporting. But never had they moved such a massive piece and today the job seemed more gruelling than ever. Chung understood the angry looks that flashed between Yuen and the apprentice. Bad joss is all you get with old things. Evil spirits lived in this piece, for sure.

The stairway was narrow. The walls and stairs ran with condensation and the air hung about the men's shoulders like a damp blanket. It took all their concentration to keep the cabinet from crashing down and as they paused at the second floor to get their breath, Chung felt the muscles in his back begin to tighten.

At the fourth floor Yuen and the lad were keen to press on, in case pausing at such an unlucky floor brought further bad joss, but at the fifth, Chung insisted on another, longer rest. By the sixth, his skin was patterned with rivulets of sweat. Even the apprentice's breathing rasped in his chest. Chung took out his handkerchief and wiped the moisture from his face.

After that they paused on every floor to ease their straining muscles. Chung wished he hadn't left his jar of tea behind in the truck as his mouth was dry and his head was pounding with dehydration.

A rack of drying washing blocked their way on the seventh floor and a tangle of bicycles on the eighth. By the tenth floor Chung was looking for ways to take his mind off the pain that tore at his chest and limbs.

Just as he felt that his lungs would explode, they heaved the cabinet up the final step to the twelfth floor. Chung leaned heavily against the bell at the back door of the apartment. A *gweilo* answered. He was tall and milk-pale with thin, light coloured hair. His manner was sharp.

"You're late," he said. "I expected you an hour ago." The foreigner led the way through a modern, hard-edged kitchen to the sitting room.

"It's to go here," he said, indicating a clear space opposite a window that gave the perfect Hong Kong vista: a view over the highrise blocks of Mid-Levels and down to Victoria Harbour. The apartment had perfect *feng shui,* facing the sea with the mountain to its back, yet the room was filled with white, glossy, flat-packed furniture made from chipboard and plywood. A single white leather sofa was positioned before a vast TV screen. Yuen and the apprentice smiled their approval.

My cabinet doesn't belong here with this *gweilo* and his shiny, new furniture, thought Chung. It should stand on a waxed wooden floor, not cold marble tiles.

A smell of fresh coffee filled the apartment, accentuating Chung's thirst. He thought of the tap in the stainless steel kitchen but before he could ask for some water the *gweilo's* mobile rang. The man disappeared into another room, closing the door behind him, leaving the men to finish the job.

Out on the landing they manoeuvred the cabinet up to the back door.

"*Aiya*. It still won't fit," said Yuen as he squatted down on his haunches, his face grim with frustration.

Chung eyed up the angles, running his hand around the doorframe.

"If we take the door off we'll gain an extra couple of inches. That might do it."

Wearily, they tackled the challenge anew, each man pulling a screwdriver from his tool belt and stepping up to the heavy wooden door.

Chung was right. With the door off there was just enough room for the piece to be inched through. An explosive sigh escaped his lips.

The *gweilo* returned as they were easing the cabinet into position.

"You've finished. Just in time. I have to go out now." Arms wide he ushered the men back through the kitchen to the rear staircase before disappearing again into the interior of the apartment.

"*Diu lei*," Chung cursed under his breath. At least the *gweilo* could have offered them some water, after hauling the cabinet up twelve flights of stairs. Even the young apprentice had more respect for his elders. Chung felt a hot fury build up inside, raising his body temperature even further.

Like a movie on rewind the men again laboured with the door, Yuen and Chung bracing it in position while the lad worked with a screwdriver, fixing a screw in each of the hinges. Pain once again shot from Chung's lower back, up his spine and into his shoulders. He could tell by the scowling face of his companion that Yuen was also feeling the heat and the strain.

Three screws, one in each hinge plate, were enough to take the weight of the door. Chung stepped back and straightened his shoulders.

"You go down to the security post and get a drink," he said. "I'll finish off here."

After the men had gone, he squatted against the wall and ran his tongue around his lips. He was so thirsty his tongue seemed to have doubled in size, filling his mouth, clogging his throat with its dryness. He sat there and waited for his pulse, his temperature and his anger to subside.

A heavy rain had begun to fall by the time Chung got back to the truck. Instead of swinging himself over the tailgate, he climbed up into the cab, pushing the lad into the middle. They glared at him as he slaked his thirst with his jar of tea.

Maybe they would treat him with proper respect after this. It may take a week or even a month but eventually everyone would find out. Or maybe this really would be his final delivery. Either way, he was too tired to care.

On the drive back, Yuen and the apprentice shared tips for the next race meeting at Sha Tin. Chung ignored them. He stared out at the rain and fingered the nine screws still in his pocket.

Andrea Brittan

A Delicate Balance

I'VE GOT TO tell you, Abigail, we were pretty freaked out by the bats at first. Bats in the wardrobe, bats in the kitchen cupboards, bats underneath the sink; wings brushing our faces at unexpected moments, the acidy stench of droppings on the carpets. At dusk the bats pour out through the attic window. At dawn they return in a quick, whispery breath.

We've come to recognize certain ones by a scar or a tear on a wing, or by their favourite sleeping spot, like the one who settles next to my head each morning, hanging from the wooden frame of my bed. Adam says we shouldn't get too attached but I name it Zachary, anyway, after your hamster, who I'm sorry to tell you died a week after you left. Zachary the bat peers at me upside down with his tiny bright brown eyes. His ears move independently of one another.

The mess would probably drive you mad. So would the scientists camping in the garden. They've set up a sort of make-shift lab, and we bring them out a constant supply of tea. They seem quite excited by our bats.

"Trans-dimensional bats are like antibodies," says Yujin. "They're a vital part of a delicate eco-system. Not sexy, but necessary." Adam's already fallen a bit in love with her. She says it takes between seventy and a hundred and thirty bats to balance one person, though they're trying to work out the variables. Things balance out in the end, that's how the universe works, say the scientists.

We're beginning to wonder how true that is, though.

Do you know how rare stumbling through a trans-dimensional portal is? You've got better odds of getting struck by lightning (one in twelve thousand) or winning an Olympic gold (one in six hundred thousand), *that's* how rare.

"And coming back?" we ask, "How rare is that?"

No-one has ever come back.

The scientists are quick to point out that there's no reason why someone couldn't – eventually, hypothetically – return, but I want them to be unequivocal, because then you'd come back just to prove a point, like that time you hitchhiked across Russia in December, after everyone told you it was mad.

If anyone's going to come back, it's you.

Your housemates miss you, Abigail. We miss you on Saturday mornings in our dressing-gowns watching shows about cake. We miss you down the pub where we never win the quiz any more with just two of us. We should move out of this house and get on with the business of being grown-ups but we just don't seem to be any good at it. You were the grown-up one, the one going places, as my mum would say.

Luke came round again last night. He left a bottle of expensive wine. "Just tell her I was here," he said. "Tell her I miss her."

Usually, the bats disperse after about three months; the time it takes for the balance to reassert itself. Our bats have been living with us for five months. It's hard to remember what the house was like before it was full of small furry bodies, stirring and opening a lazy eye as you walk past them. It is never quite completely quiet.

Here's what we've learnt about bats:

In Buenos Aires a school bus drove through a portal. The next day the parents came to the school with shotguns and killed all the bats, leaving them standing knee-deep in furry bodies, in corridors decorated with posters about summer holidays and the photosynthesis cycle. Killing the bats didn't bring the children back, but it did open up a sink hole in the middle of Via Santa Maria, swallowing several houses and a passing ambulance. This could have been a coincidence, the scientists pointed out, when they were interviewed at the scene, but you could tell they didn't believe it.

In Beijing a senior member of the politburo went through a portal. The government hired scientists to prove that the bats which occupied his government apartment were of a superior quality appropriate to such a public figure. In a press conference the scientists suggested cautiously that there were signs the bats were unusually clean, and that they arrived in an orderly fashion.

I wonder if our bats say anything about us. Anything about you.

I can say it now – we hated Luke.

We hated how he'd cook dinner for us all and tell us stories of his daring exploits in the army; how he'd buy all the ingredients from Waitrose, even the olive oil, because he used to live in Italy and said that you couldn't go back to the cheap stuff after that. We hated how we'd come home from work and find him chopping shallots in the kitchen, or reading the newspaper in the living room, his feet on the coffee table. And we especially hated how he'd say, "Don't mind me."

We minded. We wanted you to come to the pub, Abigail. We wanted you to come to karaoke at the sleazy karaoke bar and for you to laugh when Adam sang 'Valerie' to you. We wanted you to tell Luke that you didn't care if he thought it was stupid.

I thought about Scarborough the other day. Remember? That time we drove there in the middle of a storm because you wanted to swim in the sea, "Because it's the only time it doesn't feel like it's about to freeze your balls off." I wasn't convinced, but I was so happy you wanted us to go together, so happy that you were happy, at least for a while, that it seemed to me that the trees were raising their arms in welcome, beckoning us on. And you were right – the waves were weirdly warm and just as we were trying to get out, spluttering, falling back down, we looked up at the Grand Hotel and saw that stream of little dark shapes, rising into the air, flooding into one of the upstairs windows. Little shapes that came from nowhere, that burst into the world as if a door had been opened in the sky. I looked over at you, and I think perhaps you were crying.

Abigail, I just don't know what to think anymore.

Last night we gave Yujin too many gin and tonics and she burst into tears and told us they're not getting as far as they'd hoped.

"Fuck-all," she said. "That's what we've found. Absolute fuck-all."

Me and Adam said, yeah, the bats are pretty boring. They come, they go, they sleep, they shit. We didn't say anything about the gifts.

Are you sending us gifts, Abigail?

When I prised the earring out of Zachary's claws I thought he must have picked it up from a bird's nest or something. But then I thought… I know this – this little silver dragonfly with filigree wings. You wore a pair like it all the time.

Wishful thinking, Adam said. But he couldn't explain away the second gift, the little paper clip figure, the one just like all the little men that you made when you were bored in meetings. We've put it on the mantel piece in the living room, and occasionally the bats fly over to it, as if to check it's still there.

The little figure is raising his arms.

Luke just missed you so much, Abigail.

It was early Saturday morning when we heard the hammering at the door. I knew who it was, so put my head under my pillow and tried to go back to sleep. The bats had just returned and were settling down, shuffling around with contented little noises. A while later there was the smash of a bottle, and someone shouting from across the road. I heard Adam stomping down the stairs and shouting through the door. Silence. Then the sound of stones being thrown at your window, like some lovesick fifties teenager. I gave up trying to sleep. We tried reasoning. Then we tried threatening. We called the police, who talked to Luke in a fatherly way, and afterwards he wandered off down the road, then came back half an hour later with a hammer.

He probably didn't need the hammer, to be honest. The front door's still not fixed so a good push with the shoulder would have done it. He stank of booze. "Where the fuck is she?" he said, admirably coherently for someone who was swaying so much.

"We don't know," we told him. "We don't know any more than you do."

He barged past us then recoiled from the bats hanging from the clothes horse. "How can you live like this? Don't they make you sick? How can you share your house with them when they replaced her? They shouldn't be here."

And before we could react he'd reached out and grabbed one. "I'm taking it to some, some *real* scientists...not those *hippies* out there." The bat struggled in his grip and started emitting little high-pitched sounds of alarm. Those around us started waking up.

"Let it go," I said. "Please, just-"

"It's *vermin*," he shouted, and I was horrified to see there were tears running down his cheeks. "It's not even properly alive, for all you know. It's-"

He was squeezing it tighter, and tighter. I made a grab for him but he shoved me back so hard I fell against the table and Adam was shouting and the squeaking was getting louder and Luke took the bat's neck in his other hand and twisted, hard.

There was a long, slow moment when nobody moved.

Luke opened his hands and the small body fell onto the floor. "It's what they deserve," he muttered.

We stared at it. And as we stared we became aware of movement around us, of a rising noise, of the sound of wings.

We realised what was going to happen quite quickly, though it took Luke longer to understand. But when it happened, it wasn't quick at all.

I'm sorry, Abigail.

But not that sorry.

Adam and I went out of the house and closed the door and sat on the back wall. The neighbours' tortoiseshell cat wandered over to wind in and out of our legs. We didn't look back through the windows.

After a while, we finally went back inside.

It was very quiet. There was surprisingly little left of Luke.

And there was no trace left at all of the bats. No little brown bodies hanging from the bannister, no chitters or snuffles. We opened all the cupboards and wardrobes. We went and checked in the attic. But the bats had gone, they'd all gone, and I felt a black, gaping loss that hurt so much it made me dizzy.

I leant against the wall until the darkness at the edge of my eyes receded. And when that happened I finally noticed that there was something strange about the walls. I pressed my hand to our peeling, wood-chip wallpaper and felt leathery warmth. I took Adam's hand and walked into the living room. Beneath our feet the carpet moved, almost imperceptibly, as if it was breathing.

"Things leave," said Yujin, once, one night when we were sitting in the back garden as the bats poured out. "That's just what the universe does. Things leave and then other things move in to take their place and it balances out in the end." I think she was trying to make us feel better.

Things leave, but our bats are still here, in the carpets and in the walls, in little black eyes that sometimes open in light fittings and mirrors. We wonder if the balance has been restored. We wonder what the bats are waiting for. We wonder if they know where you are, Abigail.

The house chitters and fidgets at night. We lie in our bed and listen to breathing that isn't our own.

Sarah Brooks

They Were the Only Ones Dancing

I WASN'T THERE myself but my neighbour told me all about it. Things like that stick in your mind, he said. And he'd seen many things in Peckham during his many years. They weren't from around here, he said. He never used to think of me as local but what with all the table tennis bars, rooftop cocktails, and artisan flour dusting the shop fronts, he must have decided ten years in the flat above him meant I'd served my apprenticeship.

It was gone eight o'clock, another Friday night in The Hope (between the phone shop and the halal butchers), when it happened. A hotter than usual May evening. Paving slabs creaked in the heat, pigeons bathed in dust, and buses glinted with reflections of the setting sun streaked across their windows. Darkness was coming to Rye Lane but it wouldn't bring any relief from the concrete and brick soaked heat.

My neighbour was sitting on his usual stool, second from the right; far enough away from the fruit machine that the rattle of silver wouldn't remind him of the sound his settling dentures made when dropped into the tumbler at night. The daylight never quite pierced the greasy windows and thick red upholstery of The Hope; he squinted into the bottom of his glass. A draught scratched the untrimmed hair at the back of his neck.

He downed the rum; swivelling around on the stool to face the door. Three blokes, in running shoes with soles so white they must have been scrubbed with bleach, strutted in. They wore a uniform of white t-shirts and dark jeans. It wasn't anyone he knew. My neighbour tapped his foot on the rung; he'd wasted his last drop in the hope of a free top-up.

He had been chasing Guinness with Navy Rum at The Hope for going on twenty years. The other drinkers at the bar had been there for nearly as long. He used to go every Tuesday, Friday, and Saturday lunchtime, with his wife. After she passed he always stayed until late.

Surfacing onto Rye Lane in the early hours took some swift footwork, even for those who hadn't had two or three shorts to keep off the chill. All along Rye Lane, butchers took right of way. Meat stock arrived early in the morning, wheeled in supermarket trolleys, hoisted out of white vans. Beef carcasses and goat legs piled on newspaper and wooden pallets. Sidestepping deliveries was the closest anyone got to dancing on those streets. So much life already lived before the papers arrived, before the station opened, when birds nestling on the edges of Rye Common welcomed a false dawn, confused by the orange pulse of the streetlamps. My neighbour liked a lock-in.

And that's when I usually heard him, when yesterday edged its way towards tomorrow. He played records until the grey dawn trickled through his nets; sepia tinted, unwashed since his wife died. The crackle of the needle sounded like cicadas, the tropics come alive in Peckham. Mento, ska, blues, weaving threads of walking bass, and high rhythms; rising up into my dreams.

The pub jukebox was all Foster and Allen, Elvis Presley, my neighbour said. Nothing was playing that night in May, just the *ding ding* of the fruit machine. But the jukebox was in the middle of the pub, between the brown varnished tables and the brass studded bar. Whenever new blokes made a play for the place, setting out to own it, they started by controlling the music. That was what those three youths in bright whites and dark jeans did. They went and stood by the jukebox.

My neighbour said gangs came and went, and weren't they all after the same thing – a nice, quiet place to sup? White curls, a dent in the stool padding that perfectly matched his rear, meant his orders always got served and his routine never got disrupted. He thought he'd seen it all from that stool, but before the night was through he would be proved wrong.

Those youths leaned against the jukebox, not ordering, not even speaking. A quick glance at the bar satisfied them that the landlady Cheryl, and the three old timers lined up like milk bottles next to my neighbour, weren't worth a second look. The three blokes jostled against each other and the box; rearranging an elbow, straightening a knee, puffing out a chest. They eyed the tables, stretched in a line from the window to the bar.

A hot Friday night in May and the place was nearly full. A mixed crowd of those waiting to catch the number twelve bus to a club, those set for a heavy night of pint after pint, and the quiet drinkers out to escape the silence of their own four walls. It wasn't just men. Women in sleeveless tops, with strong arms and wide backs took their share of seats; toes and ankles out for spring, budding like bright primroses in the park.

One of the young blokes came back to the jukebox with three pints wedged between his hands. They drank. The men at the tables were starting to turn, ears burning, necks itching – knowing they were watched. My neighbour was about to get back to his *Racing Times*, order another rum, when the door opened. A couple came in.

Something about those two made him lean back against the bar, loosen the button behind his tie like he'd just eaten rice and peas, dumplings, and curry (heavy and sweet – just how his wife used to make it). The couple were arm in arm. Her in a flowering rose tea dress, him in a blue checked waistcoat and yellow shirt.

The way from the door, past the tables, into the pub was narrow. The couple stepped closer together rather than pull apart. Her silver patent shoes pooled like mercury waiting for the temperature to rise. The couple headed for the jukebox. The man's thin waxed moustache coming to light under the beams above the bar. My neighbour couldn't hear what the couple said, but the three blokes at the jukebox sniggered, gulped down the last of their drinks. The blokes shifted a little to the left, and the couple took their time scrolling through song titles.

A Big Band tune thumped to life. The couple placed their hands on shoulders and hips, merging together. Feet finding a rhythm, clicking and tapping on the parquet. The brass trim around the carpet made them step off each time they came to an edge, like waltzers spinning round and round the square of exposed floor.

They were the only ones dancing.

Their Peckham wasn't his, passing like ghosts – was it always that way? The dancers held each other close, the music played. They circled in and out of the flashing beams of the jukebox; cartwheels of red and green like out of control traffic lights – stop/go/stop/go.

One of the blokes, with a cockerel emblem stitched to his t-shirt, thumped the jukebox with his fist. But the music didn't stop. Some of the men at the tables began to point and laugh. They rubbed sweat and gelled hair back from their foreheads.

All that rage circling like water stains on the tabletops, but the dancing couple didn't notice. They didn't know they were watched, they didn't know the pub bristled. Their temples touched. My neighbour thought, even above the electric hiss of the jukebox, he heard that meeting of skin and skin, soft and damp as a kiss.

The dancing couple weren't listening to the orchestra of teeth sucking, knuckle cracking, lost as they were in the rhythm of the dance. One of the young blokes, with razor cuts in his hair and pumps that looked two sizes too big, made a move towards the tables. He stepped onto the dance floor. A chair got knocked backwards. A man at the tables jumped up. They stared at each other like dogs in the street. Each thinking himself cock of the walk.

Well, it's funny, that sort of posturing, until it's not. My neighbour didn't know who threw the first pint glass. It smashed on the hard wood floor, skittering shards. The dancing couple stepped apart, caught either side of the men. They looked around them for the first time. They didn't know there were places you shouldn't go into, they didn't know you should never walk in the front without knowing how to get out the back.

My neighbour stood up, not to break apart the fight, but to tell that couple, Keep dancing. Please, keep dancing. But no words came out. He grasped the velvet covered stool. It couldn't hold him. Hot striking pain, scorching him from hair roots to toes; felling him like a lightning struck London plane tree.

Before my neighbour slumped to the floor, he saw the dark chimneys of Tilbury dock, standing tall like stripped palm trees, he saw the steam fair swings rise high above the Rye, he saw grass flood the Grand Surrey Canal submerging it into Burgess Park. So many things he saw, but the last was that dancer's patent leather shoes, sparkling silver. In those he saw himself reflected, not as an old man, but as he was once: dancing close with his wife, burning bright.

He told me all about it when I visited him at King's College Hospital. I went the first time out of pity. I took in his post, watered his spider plants, brought him grapes he didn't eat, and Lucozade that he spilled on his flannel pyjamas. The green blanket was tucked tight around him, pinning him. His hands were free. The left floated above the sheet, moving like a branch in the wind, fingers tapping air as he described everything to me. How her silver shoes glistened, not crinkled like foil but bright and clear as a mirror. How the thin hairs of the man's moustache, must have been brushed smooth with a toothbrush – a redness to the tips like the henna his wife had used on her hair.

I visited him on the ward every evening that week. When he spoke about the dancing couple, about the pub, about the thrown glass, he held my hand in his right hand. We'd done no more than smile in the common hallway before that. I asked him about how the dancing couple moved, about how they held each other close. I wanted what they had, and like a patient teacher he told me all he knew.

On my last visit he pulled me close, whispered in my ear, Don't stop dancing, don't ever stop.

The second stroke took him in the early hours of the following Saturday. No fighting it, no re-generation for all.

There was a wake at The Hope, but no one mentioned the couple who had danced so close, how her silver shoes shone and his waxed moustache was polished as the counter top. Perhaps they were the only ones to have ever danced on that square of parquet between the sticky topped tables and the fruit machine.

By the time the barista and the potter moved into the downstairs flat, I had changed my walk home from the accounting office. It took an extra seven minutes to go past the pub doors but I did it each day. Every time I paused to stare through the windows at the velvet bar stools, the hardwood floor, the dark red centre of the place.

I never saw any dancing.

The Hope is gone now, refitted as a Paddy Power betting shop. And my neighbour, he's buried in Nunhead Cemetery, beside his wife. I rescued his record collection from the skip, uploaded those crackling sounds to my iPod. When I lie in bed, listening to Prince Buster's 'One Step Beyond' or The Skatalites 'Freedom March', through the window I can see the green graveside trees waving. We'll be neighbours again one day.

Emily Bullock

The Memory of the Day

H E'S NOT SUPPOSED to come anywhere near the school. Joey told me. He's only supposed to come to visit us up in Uncle Tommy's house. And that's only on Sundays. And not even every Sunday, just some Sundays. Mam would throw a fit if she knew he was here waiting for us.

Joey started in the Community School this year. But after school he's supposed to wait for me by the gate coz I'm too small to walk home on my own. The gate is where Daddy's car is parked. He's not supposed to be parked there. But when I get up to the car I can see that Joey's already sitting in the front seat so I get in. There's a smell of burn.

"Hey Joey," I say.

Joey's all quiet today. So I start kicking the back of his seat. "Quit it!" he says. Daddy's not saying anything either. He just starts driving. Usually he winks at me in the mirror but today he doesn't. Mam told Joey he was to stop calling him Daddy coz it'd only confuse me, which is really stupid. The time we visited him in the rest home we called him Daddy. He had a breakdown and he was wearing a dressing-gown and his face was all scratchy coz he didn't shave for ages. A breakdown is when you stop speaking to anyone. But that was back when we were still living up in the big house.

Daddy used to be a developer. I don't remember that time but everyone says that's what he was. A developer is when you build houses. Miss Flanagan told the class he used to be the biggest developer in all of Leitrim. That's how come we had such a big house and everything. But then it all went wrong and then Mammy took us to move in with Uncle Tommy. That was after Daddy had the breakdown.

Before Joey went to the Community School he was always

getting into fights with the twins from the Riverside estate. "Your Da's not such a big-shot now, is he?" That's what they were always shouting at Joey. The Riverside estate never got finished and all the families had to be moved into a hostel coz the toilets didn't flush properly. One morning when we were supposed to be going to school someone smeared poop all over our front-door. Mammy was crying and shouting at Daddy and she wouldn't let us go to school that day.

Uncle Tommy's not our real uncle. He's Mammy's friend. But we always called him Uncle Tommy. He used to work for Daddy but he doesn't any longer. We've been living up in his house ever since the bank took the big house back. He's all right I guess, except for when he fights with Joey. Once, he smacked Joey twice on his behind and Mammy shouted "Don't you dare touch that child!" Joey was shouting "You're not my dad" and then he bit him on his hand and he wouldn't let go and you could see afterwards the mark. That's when Uncle Tommy smacked him. After that he was locked in the room until he said he was sorry. But I don't think he ever said it.

We're not going up to Uncle Tommy's now so I ask: "Where are we going Da?" Daddy just looks at me in the mirror. He doesn't say anything. There's black on his face, like soot or something. And there's black on his hands as well. That must be where the smell of burn is coming from. Joey's just looking out the window. I suppose we're going for a drive. But then at the sign we take the turn for the lake so I suppose we're going to the lake. When Joey was little Daddy used to take him down to the lake all the time. He has this boat down there and sometimes he used to allow Joey to row. I was always too small, but sometimes he used to allow Joey. He even allowed him to hold the motor with Daddy's hand on top of his hand.

The pier is all bockedy but still you can walk on it if you're careful. That's where the boat is tied up. It's all wet and Daddy says, "Jump in and bail her out, there's a great girl." To bail is when you throw out the water with a tin of soup. There's loads of water in it coz no-one's taken it out for ages and it's all rusty coloured. When

I get in the boat it rocks and the water sloshes about, but then when I sit down it stops and you can hear the waves against the bottom. "The gossipy waves," Daddy used to call them. Mammy told Uncle Tommy he was always queer in the head.

Joey doesn't help me to bail coz he's to help Daddy carry stuff out of the boot. He needs Joey to help coz there's a basket with loads of stuff in it and a plastic can of petrol and the motor which is really heavy and has this propeller at the end and Daddy's rifle case. It's green and has straps. Joey is looking at Daddy kind of funny after he gives him the rifle case. "Why do we need the gun?" he says. "We'll shoot a few rabbits."

"Where?"

"On the island." He rubs Joey's head but Joey crinkles up his forehead and speaks at the ground.

"There's no rabbits on the island," he says.

"We'll see," says Daddy. That's what he always says when you ask him for something but then afterwards he always says yes. Or nearly always.

I'm not big enough to take any of the things so Joey has to get into the boat to take them. It rocks when he gets in. Daddy passes the basket down to Joey and then he passes the plastic can of petrol and then the rifle. "Be careful with that," he says. "Lie it down on the floor." He looks all serious like when he used to get letters from the bank and everything. Then he gets in and the boat rocks all over the place. The motor is too heavy even for Joey and he has to take it off the pier himself and then he has to tie it on so it doesn't fall off.

I put my foot on the rifle case. It's heavier even than an oar. Daddy used to go hunting with it when we were still up in the big house. One time he took Joey with him and they shot a rabbit. There was this big scab on its head when he hung it up in the garage. Mam threw a fit when she found out he'd taken Joey with him. "Jesus are you trying to kill the child?" That was ages ago though.

Daddy's elbow has to pull at the engine loads of times before it starts and then there's this big blue cloud and the engine goes thug

thug but then when we start to move out into the lake it sounds more like a lawnmower and the boat tilts up. The water's brown and there's a long line of yellow bubbles behind us so you can see where we came from. We're headed for the island in the middle of the lake which has all trees on it. Joey told me they went out there a couple of times to catch eels. It's hard to see where the rabbits would go though. It's only the same size as the schoolyard. And anyway it's going to get dark soon and then you wouldn't be able to hunt rabbits. One time when it got late I asked Daddy how come the lake was full of bright. Daddy just messed my hair. "It's bright with the memory of the day," he said.

It doesn't take long to get to the island but then you have to be careful coz it gets all shallow and there's mud and branches and rocks and reeds. Daddy steps into the water and it comes up past his knees. There's a cloud of midges around his head and everything through it looks blurry. Midges make you itchy. But the midges are coz it's getting dark. Daddy lifts us out of the boat and onto the island, first Joey and then me. But when I ask does Mammy know we're out here he says "Your Mammy's fine, don't worry about your Mammy." And I'm not. But Joey has a strange look like I've seen him sometimes when he thinks Uncle Tommy is telling us fibs or something.

Daddy pulls a big towel out of the basket. "Put that around your shoulders Katie *a pheata*," coz on the boat I started shivering. He sounds all hoarse, like when you have a sore throat. It's still not all that cold but I put the towel around me and I sit on the basket and swing my legs. "You wait here *a leana* won't you?" he says and he nods to Joey to come on.

"Where are we going?" Joey asks. Daddy doesn't say. He just puts his hand on his shoulder and then he leads him off into the woods. When Joey looks back at me he looks scared.

They're gone for ages. It's starting to get darker now. After a while a car comes beside the pier where Daddy's car is parked. It's far away but you can hear it like it's close. It's a white police car like the one Sgt O'Meara drives. She's a Ban Garda. Once she had to come into the school when someone broke all the windows of the big house. But maybe it's not her, it's too far to see. "Daddy!" I call. There's a lump in my throat because I'm crying and my nose is runny. "Joey!"

When they come back Daddy's face is all wet. His eyes are red like he's been crying too. He doesn't have the rifle with him. And even though it's dark I can see that Joey is all white and his eyes are big and he's shaking like when he's been in swimming and there's a wind afterwards. I run over to him and stick my head into him. "Take Katie back over Joey," says Daddy and his voice is even more hoarse now. And then we all get into the boat. Then after he starts up the engine Daddy gets back out of the boat. "Tell your mother…" he says. But he doesn't tell Joey what he has to tell Mammy. Then he pushes us away. "Da!" I call him. "Are you not coming Da?" But he's not. He just goes back into the woods without looking back at us.

All the way back to the pier Joey is shaking. He won't say anything even when I ask him how Daddy's going to get back. He just looks past me. "But how is Daddy supposed to get back?" and I kick his foot because I'm crying but he still won't look at me. Over Joey's shoulder I can see the trees on the island are moving up and down. They look like cardboard coz it's dark. Then the sky over them goes black with crows. Then there's this bang. You can hear the echo roll all around the lake.

David Butler

Tea and Sympathy

I WAS PLEASED that the vicar had come. He didn't go out to visit just anyone, this fellow. You either had to be someone worth sucking up to, like that woman from the big house with her pearls and her fussy little dog, or you had to be at death's door.

Lucky me.

I was never worried, mind: not even when the hospital said they were keeping me in a few more days. I was more feart of that MRSA than I was the pneumonia: my Bill was in and out with his lungs enough times that I knew the difference between a bad bout and a nuisance. But I admit I didn't contradict people when they assumed the worst, which some folk are always keen to do. Plus, I was stuck on the ward long enough to get some thinking done.

Didn't see the vicar while I was in there, though. I wouldn't have cared, if it wasn't that Mavis Johnson had seen him – twice – doing his shopping in that Waitrose they've put opposite the bus station in town, just along from the hospital. And not just an impulse, popping in for a little treat. The full weekly shop, she said! In *Waitrose*: I ask you. It's well seen he's high church.

He seemed disappointed that I answered the door so quickly: he was probably hoping I'd be too sick to get up. Clearly, I wasn't at imminent risk of dropping dead after all, but it was too late for him to dash off and find someone more important. He wasn't bright enough to come up with an excuse on the spot.

"How *are* you?" he asked, head tilted to one side, and though I couldn't really see it any more (not with my eyes), I knew he'd be pulling that sympathetic face he wheels out for any occasion that might warrant it. Too busy making sure he looks compassionate to pay the slightest bit of attention to what anyone's saying.

When he spoke at Bill's funeral, the eulogy was awful. Embarrassing. The few days following Bill's death, I'd had nothing but platitudes out of him, though I'd thought little of it. We'd been going to that church fifty years, and the vicar had been there a good five. He *knows* Bill, I thought. Bill was never a shy man: if he had an opinion about a subject – and he usually did – he'd let you know. He didn't approve of some of the changes the vicar had brought in ("the new vicar", he always called him, which I suppose should have been a warning): he thought the vicar had introduced too much fuss and nonsense into the services. Singing the Creed; that had Bill very bad, and he very rarely missed an opportunity to harangue the vicar about it.

Oh, yes, the vicar knew Bill alright.

But the eulogy he gave him; you'd think they'd never met. Nothing more than a line about his time on the PCC; no mention of all the local history projects he'd worked on. Not a word about Bill's years down the pit, or his help with the Harriers, or the Scouts. Not a word.

What the vicar went on and on about was the singing. Bill loved to sing. Liked nowt better. But, God rest him, the man was tone deaf. I've never been sure whether he knew and ploughed on anyway, belting out this awful racket, or if he really believed that what was coming out of his mouth was tuneful. It would have been fine if the vicar had mentioned it, and then moved on. But to belabour the point, the way he did? Any stranger hearing that speech would have come away thinking that Bill was nothing more than a boring old fool with a dreadful voice. And Bill was a kind man. Everyone understood that, even if he'd spent the last half-hour arguing with them. He'd bend over backwards to help somebody.

The funeral did make me relieved that I'd never let on that Bill had started having a few memory problems. Dementia, I'd guess, though I'd covered for him at GP's appointments, to postpone having to submit to any official diagnosis. It never advanced so that it was obvious. Maybe I wouldn't have noticed, if it wasn't for all my years as Dr Ridley's receptionist; but I could spot the signs alright. The muddles, the temper. Nothing made Bill more furious than feeling he'd made a mistake.

So we hadn't made it to church for a while, before he died. He had such bother with his lungs – thick of black muck, they were – he was easily persuaded that he'd be better off stopping tucked up in the house, or pottering in his garden if the fancy took him. We never glimpsed the vicar then, I can tell you. Being housebound really proves who you can rely on. All those people from church who took no notice of my mumbling attempts to dissuade them from helping; it humbles you, it really does. That's why I kept going, even after Bill's funeral. I could have packed it in, I felt so angry at the vicar, but I'm too old to start again in a new church, with strangers. They wouldn't want me anyway: half-blind and widowed (congregations do treasure their surviving men, you know), and with no means of getting there under my own steam. But the folk at our services are kind, or at least they act as if they are, and that's as good as the real thing.

I'm not much use down at the church, these days. I had to stop reading, once I couldn't see the words clearly. Then I took myself off the cleaning rota; said I couldn't make out all the dust and dirt. Only a slight exaggeration. Bill always tried to get me involved with the PCC, but he'd always come home so cross after meetings. I couldn't bear the thought of sitting there squirming, mortified, watching him get that wound up.

I bake, though. Lemon drizzle, chocolate sponge, fairy buns – always welcome at a raffle or at the Christmas fair, my cakes. I sometimes take one along for tea and biscuits after the service. Pure gannets, that congregation. You'd think they never got fed, though half of them'll be fresh from breakfast and only an hour or so off their Sunday dinner. The vicar's as bad as any of them, though he's not a big man. "Careful, Reverend," I sometimes say. "You'll not be fitting your cassock at that rate." And we all laugh. Except him, of course; doesn't even crack a smile.

In time, I could have forgiven the vicar's performance at Bill's funeral. What I couldn't excuse was, I suppose, quite trivial. In fact, he may well think he's doing me a kindness. He has this habit of mentioning Bill in his sermons, or in the parish notices – wherever I least expect it. And Bill's been gone eight years, so you'd think that either the vicar'd grow less fond of dropping his name, or I wouldn't feel like I've been kicked square in the chest when I hear it. If it only happened on the anniversary of Bill's death, then I'd find it easier; able to steel myself for the reference. But I'm obliged to brace myself every Sunday, butterflies churning in my guts, just in case.

People remark on it, afterwards. They think it's nice when the vicar remembers Bill. I never admit to them how it riles me, even though I took the vicar aside after he did it the first time. I said, in no uncertain terms, that hearing Bill's name out of the blue like that had upset me, and I'd prefer him not to do it again. So I don't know if he's just forgetful, or whether he's being deliberately unkind.

He was looking peaky today, mind. He kept coughing. He'd only choked down a couple of sips of tea, though he still managed a generous slice of ginger cake, which I'd baked yesterday, when I got home. The discharge nurse had warned me just to sit quietly, but I cannot be doing with that for long. Trying to read gives me a splitting head, while I was never fond of needlework (not that I could make the stitches out, now). And there's nowt on that television. A waste of space, it is. So I'd decided to do a little spot of baking.

"Are you alright there, Reverend?" I asked, leaning forward. I spoke very clearly, because he looked distracted.

He croaked something, waved a hand at his throat. His eyes were wide.

"Have a drink," I advised him, and he grabbed for his cup: it was the one commemorating Charles and Diana's wedding. I'd got it out specially, on the off chance that the vicar came round. I never cared for it, but Bill always had a sentimental fancy for the royals.

A drink didn't seem to help him, though. I watched his free hand clutch convulsively at the sofa cushion, as I noticed he'd sloshed half his tea onto the carpet, and I tutted. He should have put the cup down on the hostess trolley, instead of clinging to the handle, if he was going to start shaking like that. The sofa was lower than the armchair, so I always had a good view, looking down at any visitors. I'd finally cottoned on to why Bill always chose to sit there.

"It's funny," I said. "You coming to visit, I mean, when I'm not even that sick." I watched a bead of sweat roll down his clammy forehead. "I know you like to see parishioners, when they're close to the end. Gives you something to talk about, doesn't it, at the funeral? Makes you look important."

He gurgled something, groping wildly towards the telephone, but he was miles off.

"And despite all that, you wouldn't come and see my Bill, would you?" I said. "I asked, as well you know. And I hated doing it – begging – but Bill wanted to see you so badly, before he died. It would have meant a lot to him."

He was properly choking now; eyes rolled back in his head, a wretched, bubbling sputum spilling from his mouth. His heels drummed against the carpet. That was probably going to need a professional cleaner, now, as well as the sofa.

I'd prepared a whole long speech, but after I'd said those few words to him, I quite lost the stomach for it. It was one thing to see Bill proudly parading stiffened, contorted rats before the window (I wouldn't let him bring those sorry little carcasses into the house), and quite another to watch that stuff taking effect. Funnily enough, it had been one of those dreadful cooking shows playing while I was laying there bored to tears in the hospital, that gave me the idea. The lassie substituted powdered milkshake instead of caster sugar, and I wondered: how about trying something else?

I waited until he was quite still, before I rang for an ambulance. Then I heaved myself up, and moved the rat poison into the pantry. A silly place to keep it, the police said to each other later; especially given the state of her eyesight. As soon as anything was moved out of its usual place, why, it was an accident waiting to happen.

They were remarkably sympathetic, in the end (though funnily enough, none of the officers would accept a cup of tea). They took the body away, of course, and what was left of the cake. I was quite pleased that they removed the cup he'd used, as well: that was no great loss. And I hear that on Sunday, we're having the new curate from town to take the service.

I'm looking forward to it.

VL Cowan

The Change

ON HER FORTY-NINTH birthday, Anna Jennings awoke to find she'd turned into a chair. Her legs were sturdy mahogany that ended in a ball and claw foot; her armrests were blackened with greasy finger marks, and her back was fashioned from a single, uncompromising plank. Her seat was a thin pad of faded crewel work. She occupied a corner of the dining room. Opposite her was a chair the family referred to as 'Great Aunt Maud', partly because it came from her house, but mostly because, like Great Aunt Maud, it made people uncomfortable. Anna was Great Aunt Maud's twin.

Her family – husband Robert, seventeen year old Susy, and fourteen year old Jake – bickered in the kitchen, their words hurled like knives. The fridge door opened and banged several times in quick succession, and the cutlery drawer jangled.

"They're making me a birthday breakfast," Anna thought with relief. Once they'd clattered up the stairs with a tray and a tuneless rendition of 'Happy Birthday' and discovered that she wasn't in bed pretending to be asleep, they'd come and find her and this whole silly mess would be sorted out.

More banging. The clatter of spoons into the dishwasher. Susy crying, "Hurry up, loser!" then coat and school bag noises in the hall and the scrape of the front door. Jake and Susy's voices jousted down the path and along the street.

No birthday breakfast, then, but there was still Robert, arguing cheerfully with the radio, and then, louder: "Where are you?"

"I'm here!" Anna called. "Darling, something strange and not very nice has happened."

"You're breaking up. Here, let me see if I can get three bars."

"Please come and help."

Robert's mobile phone rang with the theme tune to 'Mission

Impossible'. His voice passed the dining room door. "Got you now. No. Yes. Fifteen minutes." He clumped about in the hallway, the door banged, and shortly after the car started and drove away.

The house exhaled, like a cat resetting its fur after an unwelcome stroking, and a profound peace descended. Never mind. They'd all be back in a few hours and soon grasp something was wrong and come to her rescue. It was quite nice having the house to herself: normally she led the scrum to be out of the door on time to get to work. Work, of course! Someone there would notice her empty chair and perhaps ring Robert to see if she was unwell, and he'd realise he'd not seen her that morning and fly home, anxiously. She just had to be patient. She dozed.

When she awoke, the light was slanting low through the curtains and the house was cold. The air was very dense; no one had yet come home and stirred it into life. It lay thickly over the furniture like a muffler. The hall clock ticked on.

She must've dozed again, because she came to with a snort as the ceiling light burst into artificial flame. Robert was shouting at Susy and Jake that they were ungrateful little monsters.

"We didn't want to go anyway!" Susy shot back. "What sort of saddo goes to dinner with their parents?"

Parent, Anna corrected. I wasn't there. They'd gone out for her birthday dinner without her, blind to the fact they'd lost a mother and gained a chair.

The TV erupted into life. She couldn't see it from her corner, but she could see Robert watching it, the dance of blue light across his face. She knew better than to speak to him during the news, so she waited until he stood and stretched to call out, "Robert? Can you hear me?"

He switched off the TV with a grunt and stumped upstairs. His footsteps crossed the ceiling, tracking from bathroom to bedroom, to the wardrobe to hang up his clothes, then across the landing to snap at Jake to get off the laptop and go to sleep. Eventually, the house sank into gentle vibrations. Anna tried hard not to get upset, and failed.

At some point over the next two days, the hall clock wound

down. She missed its steady heartbeat, the way it doled out time in never ending generosity. No one noticed the clock had died, that she wasn't there to wind it.

At Christmas, Robert's younger sister Beth came to stay with her husband Tom and small children. Anna was dragged out of her corner to accommodate Tom at the table. He was hefty and galumphing, swinging his foot while he ate and kicking her legs to splinters, and she was glad when a blanket was thrown over her and she was transformed into a fort for the children to play in. They leaked felt pens over her seat and crayoned on her back in sticky orange wax.

"How long have you had this chair?" Beth said, scrubbing at Anna's ruined seat with white spirits.

Robert shrugged. "It's always been here."

Beth stood with her hands on her hips, appraising Anna until she felt so ashamed she shut her eyes. "Hideous. No one keeps hold of these knackered bits of old furniture any more."

"They only come out at Christmas," Robert agreed. "They're just in the way the rest of the year. Time to get rid."

A man came from the auction house and hauled Anna and Great Aunt Maud onto a van and drove them away. At the other end, they were unpacked and labelled with a sticker bearing the number 361, and set at the end of a line of unwanted chairs. Anna's neighbour was a huge smelly sofa with its stuffing hanging out. No one spoke. Each day, a spotty youth trailed up and down the line with a broom, shunting the dust from one side to the other and never taking any of it away.

On viewing day, she was pawed by a great many people: men who turned her upside down to examine her joints, and women wearing too many rings who rapped at her frame and tutted. There was a great deal of head shaking and sucking of teeth, and at the end of the auction, she and Great Aunt Maud remained unsold. Not antique, not stylish, not ultra-modern, not comfortable. Just chairs. They were loaded onto the van and shipped back home again, and she resumed her corner.

At Christmas the children were bigger and heavier. They clam-

and think and dig and all the time the sideways weather beats a tattoo on my face.

First tea of the day does not dispel the cold. Thermos pours and steam rises, time for first gallows humour, everyone is death warmed up, no joy on Monday. This cold is moving in to stay, gatecrashing bones, a brazen parasite that never breaks eye contact when it tells, "I'll put the fuck on you, road-digger."

Begin again. Eyes on Terry in the mini Cat excavator. As each man must have his nickname in the gang, so Terry is Nursery Crimes to some, a sinister label not from evil but from the mistake of once using the word 'kindergarten' as though he was Prince Edward's butler and he must not be allowed to forget this lapse but I call him Terry and all my hopes and dreams for today are cradled in his hands. Terry can stop my mind-ticking, take me off the road, out of the weather, away from my thoughts. In the winter-grip, the ice and the road and the digger and the picks and shovels leave nothing but thought.

You taught me this, Jew to gentile – *Eleh ha-devarim* – these are the words – *eleh ha-devarim,* and even though knowing you were the teacher rips me in half, I say it. These are the words. I recall watching your lips form the sentence and catching a glimpse of your tongue or of your bottom lip sliding out under your front teeth as you made the consonant sounds. Again, again I said, as I watched and then edged closer to kiss you. Jolted back into the present and implore, sweet baby Jesus, from this gentile to a Jew, grant that Terry, as he does battle with the crust that holds the hellish legions, might tear asunder earth and rip through water main or gas pipe. Our Lord, and if she's there, Holy Virgin Mother Mary and Saint James, patron saint of labourers, hear my supplication, intercede on my behalf and take me out of this unnecessary gale and unwanted drizzle. Spare me from bollocks like today.

At 1135 my prayer is heard and if inclined it is possible to measure the speed of prayer like the speed of light but inclinations and calculations are put on hold while I exult. Terry! *Gloria in excelsis Terry!* Thou art not Nursery Crimes! Oh no! Terry is a horse of a different colour, a different gravy altogether!

An escapee from Caspar David Friedrich, Terry stands above his handiwork, stares into the hole and ponders what Man has wrought. Water throws itself into the air out from the pipe like Monday pressure and the violence of its escaping catches my breath with surprise even though it's a joyous thing.

As Terry had stared into the hole the gangerman screams at Terry or possibly into the great void for all the good it does. Gangerman's forlorn hope as it dawns that there must be no more digging to-day and feels the "heartache and the thousand natural shocks that flesh is heir to." Terry smiles and gets shouted at some more for his troubles. The secrets of the earth will not be given up today.

Nothing for it. There is nothing for it. Nothing for it at all. We must at once go to the pub we passed on the way here and in three and a half minutes we are there. No one goes home or goes to the library when work ends unexpectedly.

The diaphragm between worlds is pierced as we pass from bare street to the wood and leather sacristy and feel the whoosh of central heating on our frozen skin.

And three hours later we are still there. Nearly 3pm and the day has already almost spunked its light and inside all is twilit hues, all dusks and Terry's face, opposite me, is gold and ambers from the fruit machine and he smiles. Over his shoulder a screen shows a racecourse somewhere, horse and jockey trot to the starting post and the horse's breath rises in huge puffs of steam like locomotion and I look away to Big Tom at the bar frowning and his hand rises high above his head and comes in a great arc extended and smacks down on the counter and everyone stops to look and all I can hear is the faint sound of the commentator saying that Poor Lad is six-to-four favourite when Big Tom bellows "I'll fight any fucker in here for that!" and takes his hand from the bar and underneath it is 37 pence and he bursts out laughing and a millisecond later we all join him and I think that if any of us were Oxbridge men we'd have come up with a better nickname than Big Tom.

I revisit the jukebox that we've had playing more-on-than-off since we came in. Music intoxicates like rum and the ebb and glow and the ebb and gleam of warmth and twinkling light is in my bloodstream and the music is so ecstatic but the words so heartbreaking and I start to spin slowly and then faster so the room is a carousel of faces until Ball o'Muck stops me with a hand on my shoulder and a laugh and then leaves me and I sway and listen as The Tomangoes sing '*Why do I have to carry on this way, Lord?*' and I fight back tears because for just one second everything is too perfect.

And we drink and drink in the half-light in this half-life of twilight people and I love these days more than any now as time and people career around out of control with no sense of ever going home just a determination to grasp this moment and someone says my name – Ten Bob – and passes me another and the barmaid asks Terry why I'm called that and he tells her it's because I'm the only decent member of my family, like a ten bob piece in a drawer full of threepenny bits and she laughs and her laugh is better than anything on the jukebox. And I lean on the bar and I talk to her and before I know it Big Tom and Terry and Ball o'Muck and all the others have gone and the barmaid's shift has ended and she's gone too and I'm left alone with a bloke my age serving and I think about all the time I spent chasing the sacred and found only the profane and how I destroyed myself in rooms like this and because I couldn't see your holiness and perfection I destroyed a part of you too. And I would tell you this if you'd let me.

Stagger outside, sick up in shadows unseen. The man in the shop sells me more medicine for when I get home. Wait and catch the bus, ride upstairs, and think of the empty bed. There's one other passenger who stares at me, something sly, arch, about him. Don't focus instead but cry some few small tears and then he tries to talk to me but I'm only inside my head until I look up and see he's a younger version of me – hollowed out, all love, life and light sucked out from his eyes and we are just husks or shells, empty used-up things and he calls me a cunt and punches me twice in the face and I don't do anything in case I deserve it.

Get off the bus.

Eleh ha-devarim. These are the words. Monday over.

Dominic Grace

How To Begin

MARIJA JURIĆ IS standing over me, with fresh milk in a dented pan.

"I bought him with the ring of a dead Serb." She gestures to a small goat, grazing the hillside next to her make-shift hut. "Sometimes there is a good thing to come out of death, eh?"

Marija laughs and searches my face for a response, but I'm still weary from sleep, and trying to orient myself.

Slowly, I take in the snow-capped mountains and their familiar clefts and curves – how I have missed these mountains! – hear the rumble of the Big Waterfalls as they strike the valley floor.

I last saw my village through the fading light of summer, when the green leaves deepened to flame red: it was October 1991, and I had left to begin my second year at University in Zagreb.

In the four years since, Croatia has become an independent state, a dream accomplished through centuries of blood.

Now the war is over, and I have come home.

Marija sits down on the grass beside me, and we watch the autumn sun rise over the mountains. I drink the milk from the pan, and pull a sweater around my shoulders to protect against the chill.

Through the frost my childhood home emerges, razed to the ground: amongst the ashes lie scorched cupboard doors, and blackened chunks of sandstone from the fireplace.

A rotting beehive is still in the garden, the occupants long ago having taken flight.

The number 3 sits amongst a jagged line of hardcore, which looks as if it was laid out by a drunken hooligan in the night.

"What in God's name have you done?"

Marija is amused. I can't give her much of an explanation, but it looks as if I must have been mapping the old outline of our house.

All I can remember are the yellow eyes of an eagle flashing in the dark.

And that during the night I fell into a listless sleep, hallucinating about men in masks, and *poskoci,* nose-horned vipers, sliding across the grass.

I remember that human breath no longer mists windows, and only the wind whispers gently through the trees.

"They are finding more, every day."

Marija chews a mud-flecked fingernail.

"Mama Jurić was 87, you know. Tata, he was 90. They were so fond of their garden. They used to plant onions in the spring."

She swallows hard, looks away.

"That's where I found them. Where the water had run down the mountainside and washed the earth away... onions spoiled by the birds."

My hand hovers over hers, waits a moment. I am unsure what she wants, and I pull away.

Marija was the neighbour who wrote to me in Zagreb in the spring of 1992, to tell me that she herself had seen my parents' bodies, during the ransacking of the village. Their shoes stolen and their toes poking towards the sky, as if praying for some kind of ascension.

My parents had refused to leave everything they had created: the house my father's agile hands had built from scratch, the rooms that my mother had lovingly decorated, the kitchen stove where she had fed and nurtured us; the farm, the chickens and the sheep.

Marija made the decision to flee north in the chaos, her pleas to her elderly parents falling on deaf ears. They would not abandon the family home – at their age, what would be the point? They did not want to be refugees.

How she must have hoped that, somehow, they would be spared.

Marija begins to list on her fingers other relatives who are dead or missing, and I move her gently from the topic of her own relatives to mine.

She had never been clear about whether she had seen my brother.

"He may have fled the guns," I say. "There is a chance that he's alive."

"Many bodies," she says, shrugging her shoulders, "on a black day."

Her seeming indifference makes my blood cold. I have not been able to stop thoughts of my brother – who would have been 13 then – running dazed into the woods, where the Croats had laid mines to stop the advance of the Serbian Krajina.

Marija stands and smoothes her apron. "You must bury your ghosts," she says, "before they eat you alive."

It takes courage to turn over disturbed earth.

The patch of broken ground at the western edge of our family plot rises like a turd in the early morning light.

No-one questions why I've not yet dug into this scab of the earth's broken skin; the disturbance is understood to be on my property, so the few returning villagers will respect that, but I know what they're thinking.

I would rather fly on hope's fragile wings for a little while longer.

I have seen enough bodies on TV and in the streets of Zagreb. I do not want to see the last anguished reflex of a jaw bone, teeth clenched in a final grimace, limbs jutting out at wrong angles.

I tried to reach them. But the phone lines were dead.

Slowly, a trickle of familiar faces return to the village, though the features have hardened. Their cautious eyes search mine for answers that no-one can find.

There is the touch of an outstretched hand, the stroking of an arm, as if we are reading each other's skin like braille, language dying on our tongues.

Several days ago, a newcomer to the village arrived: a wiry little woman with her stocky husband, two sacks slung over their shoulders, hoping to settle here. They have set up a makeshift hut made of tin on the lower road, near the old mill, and most of us have let them be.

New lines of blood will begin here, mingling with the old; the light will flow into the dark, and harden into scars.

But for now, we dig.

We have become termites, roaming the hillside for our nests, looking to uncover the truth of the last 5 years.

Yesterday, Ante Kovac identified his mother's body by the shreds of an apron she used to wear for baking, and the chestnut brown rosary clasped in a skeletal hand.

He re-buried her under their beech tree, where "her heart can take root and never be displaced."

And when we are not searching, the night brings a listless existence, by the glint of the watchful eagle's eye.

The fog gathers low over the mountains and creeps like a thief through the valley. Large stone houses that were once a sign of their owners' achievements now lie silenced. Concrete stairs float into the darkness, a mythical portal to the dreams of the dead.

Ghosts dance and swim on the waterfalls, whispering to each other as they loosen a boulder out of mischief.

The thin air carries a smell of mulch, the damp must flying on the wind over the mountains. But now there is a hard iron taste in the mouth, no matter how often you rinse.

At night my brother runs, his hands outstretched, his feet bare and his trousers torn. I look for him by the old stone house where our grandparents lived, where we would dare each other on to a rocky ledge by the old mill, which hangs precariously over the river below.

We would insult each other with silly names, the innocent jibes of children.

Now, I long to say his name. But it is one of so many in the dark, and every time I'm met with a shrug of the shoulders, I lose a little part of him.

Love buried deep, and still bubbling like a shameful brook.

The villagers say I must let him go. They shake their heads as they clear their land and tend to their newly dug gardens.

And tonight, it is my last chance. Perhaps the last hours I'll spend in the cocoon of false comfort I've spun for myself.

The handful of returned villagers are getting restless: aside from my parents, my grandparents are also unaccounted for.

The only termite's nest that remains unexhumed bears down at me day and night, like an ogre in the dark.

Marija's husband, Tomislav, and Ante seem to have assumed positions of unofficial authority here, fashioning opportunity from chaos, and it seems they will dig in the morning.

Capable hands.

Marija holds my hand. The sky is black and it seems as if impending rain might halt the spades. But Tomislav and Ante don't stop, even as the first droplets soak the earth. I turn away.

The spades are barely audible as they strike the ground, but it's not long before Marija's body tenses and the earth delivers up its contents.

Marija tells me: two, side by side. I do not look. Ante finds my father's cheap plastic watch and one of my mother's dress earrings.

Tomislav is certain that there are only two, both adult skeletons.

I wait whilst the spades slowly, quietly, re-fill the hole.

My grandparents are still missing, and we will have to search the wood behind their house.

The men retreat back to Tomislav's hut for beer, and Marija asks, "What will you do here now?" She looks at the light filtering through the mountains. "You are young, your whole life ahead of you. You can get employment anywhere. In one of the cities, perhaps. Those of us who are older… we've no choice but to come back."

"I'll wait for my brother," I say.

And the look she gives me is something between horror and pity. Once, no gossip passed her ready tongue; now she is defeated at last. She leaves me to join the men, and I watch her disappear up the hillside.

Winter will come soon and I will need to put together some kind of makeshift shelter; I have been too reliant on the canopy of the stars to guide me at night. Some builders from Otočac have agreed to help clear the rubble of the old house. I will find a job in the National Park, and pay them gradually to restore the house that my parents built. As the night draws close, I mark my parents' grave with a large stone from the Korana River. Their silent presence is a strange sort of comfort. Now they are safe.

I keep a candle burning on the grave, hoping it will call my brother home, an eagle's eye in the dark. Perhaps one day soon, the face that I most long to see will come over those mountains.

Stipan. That is my brother's name.

Susan Hodgetts

Already Formed

Every August my summer boy arrived on the beach. I watched him from my studio window, and sometimes I made sketches of him; a boy in Rory's image, caramel-skinned and lathe-thin, like a shaft of sunlight.

I often saw him when I went for my morning walk. A line of upturned rowboats basked in the dunes like a row of giant turtles, and he would slalom between them as he raced down to the receding shoreline.

On my return I'd find him crouched over rock pools, parting fronds of seaweed to reveal tiny crabs, his slender fingers entwined with the blood-red tentacles of anemones. At his side there would be a bucket filled with shells and freckled pebbles, their colours fading to pale as they dried in the sun.

As I watched him, I imagined my summer boy was Rory, separated from me at birth by a mistake, waiting for me to reclaim him when the moment was right. We'd build sandcastles decorated with shells, win candy and key rings on the penny falls, then walk down to Balducci's for ice cream sodas.

It was difficult to remember my life before Rory. He became mortal even before I did the pregnancy test; as tangible as if he'd already been born. He was your reassurance that you wouldn't let me down, that you'd finally tell your wife. The day I did the test you bought me the sea-green dress that shimmered, and you told me I was your mermaid. And Rory was the sound of my laugh when I threw the shopping bag onto the bed, reminding you that in a few months time I may be too big to wear it. At that moment Rory became the tangible future: just me, a baby, and a life filled with bottles and nappies. And occasionally there'd be you. But in that vision the sea was always rough, and I couldn't see the horizon for rain on the glass.

Finally he was my forehead against the cool bathroom tiles, and the knot in my stomach as I waited for the line to turn blue. And then, just like that, he was gone. Gone without touching the sides. Rory wasn't even a blue line on a pregnancy test. He was a line missing. He was your obvious relief, your pale smile, your cold fingers on my arm. He was your voice telling me that you would have been torn between this new baby and your own children. An odd thing to say: your own children. As though Rory would have been less yours in some way. As I lay awake that night, my relief changed to grief. I grieved for the inevitable end of our affair, and for the loss of the unwanted child who was already formed in my mind.

The next day you went back to being the good husband, and I went back to being the single girl.

In the holidays I still went down to my beach house to paint, half-hoping, half-dreading that you'd arrive next door just as before. You'd always used your cottage as a refuge, a place you could work in peace – no wife, no teenagers home from college, no computer games blaring. But for months on end it stood empty, the shutters battened and peeling. The following summer I heard a rumour that you were renting it out, and so I guessed you were never coming back.

The whole of July was cool and cloudy, and I became restless. Then on the first Saturday in August a dented blue Land Rover pulled up outside, and I rushed straight to the window to assess the new tenant. A woman was lifting a baby carrier from the front seat, and as she walked over to the cottage the sun appeared, exactly as though it had been waiting for their arrival. She stopped for a moment to scan the horizon, holding a hand up to shield her eyes before going inside to throw open the shutters.

She had brought my summer boy, and I no longer needed to think about you. I had Rory instead.

That first year I watched him in the cottage garden, never out of his mother's sight. When I saw them getting ready for their walk I would rush outside, clutching my trowel and secateurs. The woman hardly noticed me as they passed by, the pram dusted in fine, pale sand, and Rory dressed in tiny babygros patterned with red and blue yachts, his hair a halo of spun gold.

I was pleased that she paid me no attention, for if we had introduced ourselves, then I would have found out the boy's name too, and how could the boy be Rory if I knew he was Joshua or Andrew or Harry?

The following year I watched him take his first tentative steps. And as soon as he could walk he found the sea. Whenever his mother dragged him back he would spin straight round and waddle on his fat legs to the water's edge again. He flicked up seaweed with his neon-pink spade, giggling with glee at the stub-legged dachshund that circled him.

When he was old enough to explore by himself he conquered the beach: no stone unturned, no dune uncharted. His strong limbs carried him across the sand, fishnet trailing, tongue curled around his upper lip in concentration as he picked up starfish and hermit crabs, and cautiously touched jellyfish with the tip of his rubber flip flops. His mother would leave him to play for hours on end whilst she sunbathed or read her book.

I could never understand why she didn't want to watch him every minute of the day as I did, trailing in his footsteps, mesmerised by each perfect bare footprint, each sandcastle, each shriek of joy.

One afternoon, in Rory's eighth summer, I saw him stretched out on the edge of the slipway after a swim, his eyes closed against the sun. I wanted to touch his hair, his long pale lashes, to smell the summer heat and the sea salt on his skin. I walked on the beach at the side of the slipway, my face level with his, and stopped to watch him. I reached out my hand to stroke the smooth skin on his cheek. As my fingers hovered above his face, he sensed my shadow and opened his eyes. As he met my gaze, I was transfixed, not noticing his mother until she started to run towards us. I pulled my sun hat down over my eyes, and left the beach quickly without looking back.

I went straight to the house and up to my studio, hastily sketching. I filled sheet after sheet with bold strokes of colour, tacking them randomly to the wall behind me. I needed to capture his essence, to feel his movements through my pencil and my brush. He was the colours of the dunes: the sand, the wild flowers and the wind-blown couch grass. He was the colours of the sea: the water and the white spume beneath the unbroken blue of the sky. And more than all of those he was the colours of the rock pools: the reds, the greens, the speckled browns and pinks.

And for the first time in months, I thought of you. Where were you now? Did you ever wonder how lonely I might be? Did you imagine me with someone else, or think I'd be tied to the past, to the memories of our last day, to the son I had created in my mind?

I looked for the white carrier bag that had remained untouched at the back of the wardrobe, and took out the mermaid dress. It shimmered in the sun, and I shook the dust from its folds and stepped into it. It still fitted; a sheath of iridescent scales.

When I heard someone knocking, for a moment I imagined it was you, that I'd conjured you by thought. I rushed downstairs, running my fingers through my hair and straightening the dress, calling out to you. There were two policemen stood at the door, and stupidly I thought they had brought news of you. I probably sounded nervous when I asked them what they wanted. The younger one touched the front of his cap respectfully, and said they were sorry to bother me, that they could see I was busy. I must have looked questioningly at him, because he gestured to my hands, to the smears of yellow ochre and cerulean blue. The colours of my summer boy: of Rory. My hands were daubed with him.

The policeman kept saying something about a woman; a woman with a sunhat who was seen by the slipway. There'd been a complaint. A mother, her young boy, my neighbour. Did I know them? Had I seen anyone hanging around the beach? I shook my head and muttered my replies.

As they walked back down the path I snatched my sunhat from the window ledge and pushed it down the side of the chair. I noticed that the mermaid dress was smeared with paint and the sky had clouded over. Everything was suddenly wrong.

The next day I bought a new hat from the souvenir shop, then took a walk towards the pier, away from your cottage. The tide had just gone out, and the beach was a smooth arc of virgin sand. I wanted to be that beach and start all over again. And again. And again. Every day the sand had her slate wiped clean by the sea. She presented herself anew as if nothing had ever happened there before, as though no dog had ever left untidy paw prints in a skittering arc, as though no couple had ever written their names in the sand.

It was as I walked up the steps near the pier that I saw you. You were sat at the traffic lights on the shore road, heading towards the cottages. You didn't see me, you were too intent on the road. You looked worried, older, your hair shot with grey, and I knew for certain that you weren't looking for me. Something was wrong.

I ran back along the beach, and when I saw the car parked outside your cottage I understood. What I had seen in the boy's face was not my own illusory child, but you, and somewhere within me I had known this from the start. Because all along he was your summer boy. All along you had your own Rory, already formed, already growing, already more than a blue line. That last unplanned baby.

I went into my cottage through the back door that afternoon so that you wouldn't see me. I heard the gossip later – the inevitable stories that circulated the village. The unplanned baby, I discovered, had broken rather than saved your marriage. You'd decided – predictably – that you couldn't do nappies and sleepless nights again. It was the first time you'd been seen in the village for years. And the woman who had tried to kidnap the boy? Perhaps she had lost a child of her own? A day-tripper most probably. She was surely in need of help?

But the gossip was soon forgotten, and nothing further was said about the possible identity of the woman on the beach. Life went on without interruption.

For the next few years I still saw your son and your ex-wife when she opened up the house for those few weeks in August. When I bumped into her in the village shop, or we passed on the beach path, I sometimes said hello. She always looked puzzled, as though she could never quite place me, and then she would instinctively reach for my summer boy's hand.

Mandy Huggins

Wonderland

WE ARE DRUNK. All of us. Really drunk before we even arrive, and determined to have good time. We pile into a taxi, pile out. Run about, giggling, stumbling, between grey University buildings, and pavements, and carparks, all transformed. The grounds we know well, no longer timid well mown lawns, but filled with marquees and fair rides and rusty old swings, part festival, part end of year ball. And before long it's just me and you. Me and you, against a backdrop of coloured bulbs, and the Library's concrete sweeping stairs. We run from block to block across grass and bits of burger. This is a ball filled with popcorn and candyfloss, a fair filled with ball gowns and high heels. We whirl towards the dodgems, bashing and battering our way to victory. "We have to go again," you say, and this time you must drive. So we do, whizzing about, time after time. "I'm Alice," you say, "Alice in Wonderland". I look at the laughter on your face. Your full-throated enjoyment from a dodgem car at full throttle and I believe you.

I have planned this night for weeks. For weeks I have waited for it, hoping, hoping that it will be like this. I have fingered dresses, and practised makeup and tried to see my face each time through your eyes. I have sat frozen beside you and felt the heat from your fingers warm mine, and told myself that tonight, tonight I will. And now here we are, under a sky broken by threaded fairy lights and your grey eyes. I lean forward and grab your hand spinning the steering wheel erratically. I forget myself. Everything blurs. Everything, but me and you, and our two hands touching on a fairground ride.

"Did you have nice time?" I know that tomorrow Mum will ask this whilst standing in my doorway. She will stand in my doorway, just as she does most mornings. "Did you have a nice time?"

She will ask again. I will not answer the first time.

"Yes, it was fun," I'll say. Then, knowing this will not be enough. "They had rides as well as the dance tents, and food. I think I got ketchup on my dress." All of which is true, there is ketchup on my dress. All of which is true, it is just not quite the truth.

There are bottles and burger buns on the normally well-kept grass. We creep behind the buildings in amongst the trees. A thread hangs from your dress, swinging behind as you skip, trip, around branches in wild heady excitement. It catches, breaks, you do not notice as you catch my hand and we fall, pulled against a tree trunk. The bark grates against my back, stripping my shoulder blades, bare in the dress I took so long to choose. The air is cold, fresh, and we are stood beside two splashes of spring yellow. You tuck a daffodil into my hair, where it sits bold above the green of my dress, you joke you have grown them specially for me. Your hand soft down my face, my neck, my chest, down. Leaning back laughing I close my eyes, feeling your breath come closer, traces of salt on your lips. I know I have fallen down the rabbit hole.

I will not tell Mum any of this. Although she once told me falling in love was important, even at nineteen, especially at nineteen. She said every little bit of falling in love matters, always will. I will not tell her any of it, although I am thinking this must be what she means, because this, right here, is important. This is Wonderland.

We have a popcorn fight. Handfuls of it everywhere; in hair, down dresses, stuffed up noses and ears, all the time tumbling our way back towards the lawns, toward the dance floor. You stumble ahead dragging me through the crowd. You trip, legs long and gangly and uncertain in heels you are not used to. We wait, in a long queue to get to the entrance. Fragments of pop tunes drift across our heads, melodies and beats which make my body ready to move with yours. In front and behind people bob as they wait, uneasy, ungainly, in and out of time. Tonight I am not one of them. Tonight I am perfectly in rhythm, spun by the memory of your hand at my thigh.

Slowly we start to move forward. The heat of the crush mingles with our own, out of breath, hot and eager. Slowly we make our way towards the main marquee. You are unravelled, mud scuffed on one leg, mascara smeared down a damp cheek to your smile. Yet you are beautiful. Truly. There is no other way to see you, standing in a red dress and loosely pinned hair. Beautiful, and with me, hand in hand.

"Fucking fags."

I am sure I hear it. I am sure you hear it too although there is no acknowledgement in your face as you push your way through the crowd.

"Disgusting."

A voice from behind us. There is no change in your pace but your body tautens and you pull me harder. "Fucking fags." I'm not sure now I will ever stop hearing it. There is music still. I know there are notes breaking in the air, but my ears are thick and filled with a different echo. "Fucking fags." I am hot, angry, ready to turn and shout, to fight. Or that is how I want to feel. Instead vomit is rising in my throat and my cheeks begin to burn. Instead I keep walking. Alone now because you are just ahead. Alone now because you have pushed on and loosened your hold on my hand.

We have to wait again, the crush of the crowd stops us just as we are about to surge into the tent. I can feel them behind us. I can feel his voice burn the back of my neck and I turn to see. You, you stay staring straight ahead, you, sobered slightly, smooth your hair, straighten your dress. The smell of hotdogs is still on the air as my stomach turns. I see him stood tall in a fine suit with finer face. I see him, words hung on his lips behind us, chiselled chin, private school boy hair. He meets my gaze, he sneers. His girlfriend is with him. Stood with the pack, the crowd. She is tall, with expensive shoes and diamonds on her wrist. His girlfriend who says nothing, but leans across to stop his words with a kiss. Who giggles as her shoulder strap slips and she pulls her mouth from his. And I feel sick. Suddenly I recognise myself again, I, in dumpy dress. The stench of a burger van clung to my clothes, my hair, sweaty, stuck to my face. And you, you next to me. You, slipping your hand from mine.

We join the others, and we dance. I buy more drinks, joke, twirl. You avoid my gaze. I buy more drinks, trip over someone's feet on the journey between the bar and dance floor. We dance. I feel myself beside you, red faced and clumsy now, trying to ignore my dress which suddenly seems to pull tight across my hips, my makeup which feels loud and clownish. You make a joke and I smile into your face, and then suddenly the ground is rushing towards me. I need to be sick. I run to the front of the tent, out onto the grass. I think of your eyes at my smile, your mouth turned slightly away. I vomit again and again. Vodka mixes with bile, burning my throat, my stomach contracting until I am raw. I think of your face, plastic and ashamed, and turned away. I retch again, coughing, beside a couple who watch me in pity. Bent over, my back resting against a tent pole, I close my eyes and take deep slow breaths of fresh air.

The sky is no longer clear and spots of rain have come. I welcome the sharpness of the night. The rain drowns my burning cheeks, soaks my bowed head. The daffodil drops from my hair, I swallow, wipe my eyes, walk back to join you on the dance floor.

All night we keep dancing. I think that is what I will tell Mum in the morning, "We danced all night." And that too will be true, although not the truth.

"It doesn't matter," you eventually turn and say to me. "It doesn't matter."

"No," I agree, "it doesn't," and you touch my shoulder. But you have straightened yourself out, smoothed away all trace of desire and left me standing here alone. The music is still playing, and we are dancing just as before, but the night is broken all the same. You take my hands to twirl underneath the disco ball which seems to spin and glitter in derision. "Alice," you say, "Alice in Wonderland." We keep on dancing.

You are trying to make me smile, but your voice sounds coarse and hard, the words not the same. You are trying so hard to make me smile.

We keep on dancing, and half-pretend ourselves in revelry. We keep dancing and those words ring out between us over again and again. "We had fun," I shall say, to Mum stood in the doorway of my bedroom in the morning. Then I will ring you I think, and we will talk. We'll complain about our headaches and nausea and mouth furred with vodka and chips and toast. Maybe you'll pause and say: "Everything's a bit of a blur, but did we…?" And I'll say, don't worry we were drunk, it was nothing, and we'll laugh. Friends again. But for now we dance, and I close my eyes so I can't see the change in your face. I close my eyes and I remember the feel of your skin on my skin. And I forget the moment when you quietly dropped my hand.

Maureen Lennon

This Time

2001

He does not remember the first time he sees her, and she doesn't notice him at all.

She's on the lawn outside the Student Union, hair sunshine-spotted and a pint glass in her hand – giddy with end-of-term pleasure, like nearly everyone here. But he's three exams short of celebrating, so he swigs his coke and stares down at his book, and the next time he looks she is gone.

All these dates that won't go in, and how come everyone else is free? And why hasn't Lisa called? Is she on another lawn outside another Union, being chatted up by some lad with a floppy fringe and a posh accent? And he needs to learn these bloody dates, and after Friday he'll never open a book again unless he wants to.

She is laughing as she wonders how badly she did in that Eliot question, wishing her thighs looked better in jeans, scanning the rabble of drinkers for the bloke she met last week – Adam, curly hair and a wicked grin – all while laughing and listening to Nicky's rueful rundown of her mistakes.

It's sunshine and pissy lager and the grass prickling under her palm, and will she get a two-one and is this her third or fourth pint, and why didn't she tell Adam to ring her? And Nicky did not get all those questions wrong; they both know she's safe for a 2:1. And god, she never has to read another book again unless she wants to.

She's on the fringes of a leaving do in London, the dry ice and pills disguising the dinginess of everything except the clientele, who still have the arrogance and sheen of life unlived. Nobody else is watching their mum fade away, like she is; nobody else is arguing about care arrangements with siblings.

He's talking to Jen, her friend who's leaving for New York, and when he glances over she looks away. His hair is soft and a little long, his expression open, with friendly eyes and a sweet, confident grin that's all for her.

But Jen – witty, skinny, *New York* Jen – got there first, and doesn't he know the rules? How dare he smile at her like that, as if she'd come if he crooked his finger (oh, but she would, she would), and she'll show him, won't she? She'll make him see not everybody falls at his feet.

When he looks up she's there, an answer he didn't ask for. Like he's always pictured Anne Boleyn, with a black river of hair and wild, starry eyes, emerging from the smoke like Vivien Leigh.

But she ignores his grin, so he turns to the girl beside him, who's still talking about a job, a magazine he's never heard of, and the next time he checks, she is gone.

2004

Same bar, next year, next June: she's chatting to a friend of a friend of a friend, and there he is, beaming. "I don't think we've met."

"No." She shakes his hand, and she isn't going to sleep with him, definitely not, but hey, they went to the same university, lived round the corner from each other, and god, remember Lexy's on a Wednesday night? And urgh, the watery beer at the Union, and aren't we glad we're out of that, because we're adults now, aren't we; we're in *Larndon*, haha. Then they're outside – in a black cab, his lips on her shoulder – outside her front door, and please don't let Nicky be home yet – in the kitchen, fingers dipping under each other's clothes – on her bed, the wine glasses trembling on the bedside table, and she had no idea she was so lonely and heartsick until she isn't.

In the morning he's hungover and she won't meet his gaze. She's moving back up north, because her mum's "not very well". He knows he should hug her – wants to hug her – but the spark has faded from her eyes, leaving a hunger he doesn't want to sate. He kisses her cheek and gives her his number. No point giving him hers, she says, she's leaving in a week, and he asks for nothing else.

Sweet but needy, he tells Tom over a pint, and anyway, she's gone now. He's better off out of it, although when he remembers her she's always wearing that Anne Boleyn stare.

2010

Six years later he's married to a friend of a friend of her friend, and she's back with a boyfriend in tow. No need to be awkward around each other. She's still pretty, and if she hasn't regained that spark since her mum died, her self-assurance is even lovelier.

He and Gabby are trying for a baby, and he couldn't be happier, really, but he can still appreciate an old flame – although she's not even that. It's nothing, never mind Tom's knowing smirk; doesn't mean he can't enjoy the way she strokes the hair out of her eyes, or watch her hands skim her boyfriend's jeans and remember how they felt against his skin.

It's so lovely that they can be grown up about this. Here's Phil, beside her, and there's his wife, Gabby, who seems lovely. Really lovely. And he looks lovely, too – not as gorgeous as she once thought him, but she was young and unhappy then, and now it's just lovely, isn't it, that they can relax and actually talk?

He's got great taste in music and it's good to chat to someone who gets the references; whose eyes gleam at the mention of bands everyone else forgot years ago; who really cares about what's happening to the world like she does. And it's lovely to be comfortable, to not worry about impressing him, and really, it's all just lovely.

2012

She's single again, but doing all right, although it was tough when Phil told her he was gay. (Seriously! Who does that happen to in this day and age?)

Anyway, she's done it, learnt to live by herself; she's finally living and hurting and showing to the marrow, confident she can hold herself together.

And here *he* is, and she still has a crush on him (she can admit that now she's single, but she'd never make a move. He and Gabby are lovely together, just lovely), and they still have the same taste in music (and in books and films, and do you remember that cafe in the Student Union, and the beer festival every April? We must've passed each other in the bar all the time!). And it's probably – definitely – the wine, but when she grins at him his face lights up and the years and those around them fade away.

You're exactly what I want. The thought ambushes him and his smile falters, because Gabby – where the hell is Gabby when you need her? – he is married to Gabby and very happy, thank you.

He's betrayed himself; he sees it in her worried eyes and bitten lip. He stands up, walks with his wine until he's beyond her orbit.

When he sees Gabby, laughing on a barstool with his old friend Tom, he stops and watches. But what he's really seeing is her, behind him, hair shorter now and sleeker, but still tumbling into her eyes above that Anne Boleyn smile.

Single at thirty-five – not a situation he predicted or enjoys, although it's partly his fault and his friends have been great. Gabby's been great, although that's possibly because she's already shacked up with a bloke he's trying hard not to hate. And it's already started, the casual set-ups, the single friends dredged up from god knows where. "Just thought you two might get on…"

And oh god, it's her, and yes, she's still single – or single again – and he can't fuck this up, he just can't. But by last orders he's slurring all over her, failing to keep his hands to himself. And she's nice about it, which is worse, because she pities him and you never fancy someone you're sorry for; you just don't.

She ignores the goosebumps tracking the movement of fingers on her arm; he's drunk and she won't go there again. So she smiles and shakes her head when he murmurs in her ear that she's exactly what he wants, what he's always wanted. But she hugs him tight, because life is hard, it's so bloody hard. She kisses his cheek, lets his head rest on her shoulder, and pushes him into a cab. Alone.

2016

Tom and Gabby's wedding, and here they both are on the singles table. He's looking better, she notices – the confidence is back in his grin – and his blushing apology for their last encounter is sweet.

By the time they've toasted the bride, sharing knowing smiles over their glasses, they're swaying in and back like teenagers on a fairground ride. Words don't matter: the important part is to keep the dance going. Which is easy to do with him smiling as if she's the answer to a question he's been asking for years.

This time; this time; this time. She chats to acquaintances, laughs at the music, zigzags away for drinks, is diverted by friends, but is drawn back always to him. Finally, helplessly, he takes her hand and pulls her, or she pulls him, out onto the lawn.

Don't think; just do it. He knows it's going to happen, knows she wants it, but still his heart thuds as she looks up at him through her hair. Don't think. Don't think. She lifts her face to his, and how long is it since he kissed anyone like this? Don't think. Don't think about what's happening here; don't think about Gabby and Tom, laughing and falling into each other's arms on the dancefloor. Don't think about how you've fancied this girl for fifteen years. Her arms slide around his waist, and her lips are soft and giving, and god, her hands on his bare skin; why haven't they been doing this for years? This time, he promises himself as he pulls her closer: this time he will keep her if he can.

2016

She's foraging for breakfast in the fridge, a pint of water to clear her head and her dry lips fighting off a smile. Alone again, but the flat feels different now, as if his presence has decorated it anew.

Last night they fell into bed like students, hungry and hopeful and too happy for fear. Even if he never comes back, if he was lying when he said he'd call, she's glad it happened. If she repeats this enough it'll be true.

At the buzzer's call, she checks her reflection in the metal cooker head, but yesterday's make-up and her fuzzy dressing gown are beyond help. She opens the door with a shaky hand, and there he is, wearing yesterday's suit and a cocky grin that doesn't mask his nerves.

When he proffers the Sunday paper she kisses him hard, pulling him indoors, and breakfast over the paper is a long time in coming.

He tells her she looks like Anne Boleyn and she grins into his chest. She tells him he's too pretty for his own good, and when he reminds her that she cold-shouldered him in that London bar, she sighs.

They eat sushi and curry; they find a flat together; they dance to bands no one else remembers. He argues with her dad about Richard the Third, and she works on that novel about her mum.

They compare uni photos, playing "do you remember" and "did you know…?" And sometimes, when she smiles at him on sunny days, he glimpses a girl tilting a pint glass, laughing with her friend on a lawn twenty years away.

Elizabeth Ottosson

She Went Out for Milk One Morning and Only Came Back the Previous Day

BY THAT TIME, my brother had learned a few tricks himself. Instead of walking into the pub through the door, he unfolded from the gap between two floorboards. I had already bought the first round, so I just pushed his glass towards him.

I hadn't seen him for a couple of months, so we made small talk at first: work, my new flat, the weather. The conversation inevitably gravitated towards his girlfriend, who had recently transcended time and space.

My brother took a long swig before he spoke.

"Yeah, she's doing fine. Doing her thing, you know. She's kind of just all over the place."

"How did the family visit go?" I asked. Our parents never quite saw eye to eye with her. Her new state of being didn't exactly help.

"Oh, yeah, yeah, pretty well," he said. "Got some photos actually, if you wanna see them."

Did I? You bet I did. I hoped I didn't seem too eager.

He took out his phone and, after digging around for a bit, turned the screen towards me. He cleared his throat.

"They finally did up their garden. It looks so much better now."

I spent no time checking out the garden. My brother's girlfriend was in the foreground, right next to a table laden with coffee and cake. Her face—and not much else—hung impossibly over my mother's shoulder, grinning like the Cheshire cat. My mother's own smile looked forced, with a hint of fear in her eyes.

"Oh, this is great," I said.

"Yeah, um, I'm glad they cut the hedge back," my brother replied. "Hey, how about—"

"So you guys moved in together, right?"

He sighed.

"Yeah, we did. Just before she…" he stopped for another sip. It took him a few moments to reply. "Sometimes, I catch a glimpse of her out of the corner of my eye, just a reflection in the frost flowers of the window. I turn to tell her something, but she's gone."

"Oh." Not sure what to say to that.

"I don't actually get to see her much these days. Well, I hear from her. She sent me this text a week ago, says she's having a stroll through the fifth circle of Hell, in a garden of flowers she said smelled of hubris." I wasn't sure whether he was annoyed at her for going there or for going without him. I felt obliged to contribute something.

"Maybe you two should try doing more things together," I tried, "You know. In, um, a relationship you want a bit of independence, like each having your own thing. But you've kind of gone, like, too far the other way."

My brother waved his hand, unconvinced. "Yeah. Yeah, sure. Me, I'm definitely trying. I mean, watch this." He reached out, his hand becoming a convoluted blur. A moment later he pulled his arm back, holding a packet of salt and vinegar crisps. I glanced at the bar. The bartender reached behind his ear, perplexed, and retrieved a pound coin.

"Nice," I said.

"And her? She arranged to meet once. Sounds promising, right?"

"Right," I nodded.

"She did that with a note traced on the dirty window on the back of the bus I was running after. She wanted to meet at the Duplicate Hog Pub, five years ago. I didn't—don't even know where that is!" He swirled the beer in his glass thoughtfully. "It's unbelievable. I finally got her to join me for a picnic. Found a nice spot in the park, made some sandwiches, brought a blanket to sit on and a bottle of wine, the works. And the entire afternoon she was just… not completely there."

"Oh, like, on her phone kind of thing?"

My brother narrowed his eyes at me.

"No, I mean, half transparent winking in and out of existence every couple of seconds kind of thing." His phone buzzed. Picking it up, he said, "If we're spending time together I want it to be proper time together, you know? It's not really too much to ask, is it?" He checked the message and groaned. "Christ. It's her."

"Where is she now?" I asked, tentatively.

"She's at the CERN car park, supercolliding cars."

I tried not to laugh. I failed.

"Hey!" my brother snapped. "It's not funny! Last I heard, they were re-jigging one of the accelerator things to shoot protons *at* her."

I straightened my face the best I could, and apologised.

"This is serious, OK? I'm worried about her."

We remained quiet for a couple of minutes, finishing up our beers. I spoke first. "So have you thought about..." The million possible ways this sentence could have ended wavered and converged, forming a single, definite question... *breaking up?*

My brother thought for a moment, expressionless.

"Honestly?" he said, and then smiled for the first time that evening. "I haven't had this much fun in *years*."

He got up and offered to buy the next round, the normal way.

Andrey Pissantchev

Touched

THERE WAS A new girl in Tasha's classroom when she drifted in for Citizenship. The girl had ginger frizz-ball hair and a face crawling with freckles, but what struck Tasha more than those things were her gloves. Before she realised what they were hiding, she was mesmerised; they were clearly expensive, genuine leather, only they weren't black or brown but green.

Like seaweed, she thought, *or wet cabbage. Avocado skin...*

Tasha was wasted. She'd been holed up with Lily behind the bins all lunchtime, and Lily's weed was so strong that when the sun broke through the clouds, the tarmac exploded glitter and the Year Sevens playing football glowed like fairy-lights.

The new girl was sitting in their back row, across the aisle from Lily's desk, and though there was more sunshine swirling between them, it had nothing on those gloves. Sleek and glossy, with buttons on each wrist, they brought to mind black and white movies and femme fatales. When the girl began to inch them off, there was something glamorous and old-fashioned about how she did that too.

The girl took her time, pinching and tugging each fingertip before peeling her right glove free. The hand underneath was skinny and winter-pale, without nail varnish or rings. There was nothing special whatsoever about it, but when the girl revealed her left –

Beside Tasha, Lily gasped.

Was it even a hand? Some weird sick joke? Its proportions were so distorted that at first Tasha thought it was another far stranger glove. Slightly too large for the arm it hung from, it was dingy-grey and swollen. More than anything, roughly stitched –

The scar didn't just knit the girl's wrist but crept up towards her thumb, a dark fraying cord, the skin around it puckered. Each finger looked greasily bloated, the lumpy knuckles grazed.

But though the hand obviously wasn't the girl's own – well, not her original, at least – it wasn't a prosthetic. It was real, live, working flesh.

As Tasha stared, those fingers flexed and she shuddered, imagining blind worms nosing the dust-lit air. Apart from a freaky face transplant on Instagram, she'd never seen anything like this in her life.

"*Frankenstein*," Lily hissed.

She meant the monster not the doctor, but Tasha wasn't about to put her right. Lily's blue eyes had grown wide, their blue glazing into ice, and Tasha knew that look too well.

Sure enough, Lily leant away from her desk, shattering the sunshine, and "Frankenstein!" she yelled. "Hey, *Frankie* – yes, I'm looking at you."

After school, they followed the new girl to the bus garage. Lily had her phone gripped between her gel-clawed fingers. "Frankie," she kept calling, "give us a picture. Come on, *Frankie*... don't be a bitch."

The girl's gloves were back on – pure, green streaks, sweeping her sides as she marched ahead. She didn't turn around once, not until they reached the garage and there was nowhere else to walk. It was a mistake, obviously; within seconds, Lily had her cornered, pinned up against a wall.

Lily was stronger than she looked. Like one of those little dogs with locking jaws, Tasha thought, as Lily snatched the new girl's sleeve.

"We don't want to hurt you, Frankie," she said. "We just want a better look."

The girl's hair fanned orange across the bricks. She couldn't escape, but she didn't look about to cry. The entire time Lily grabbed at her, she kept her lips pressed tight and her chin held high, her freckled face averted. But when she briefly closed her eyes, Tasha understood. The girl was disappearing. In her head, she was somewhere else.

Then, thankfully, the bus appeared, and because it was heaving with Academy boys, Lily released the girl to turn, and flip her white-blond hair, sending the boys into full-on zoo mode, whooping like apes and thumping the glass.

Lily didn't give the girl a second glance. "Catch you later, Frankie," she called back lightly, strolling over to the bus.

That night, Tasha dreamt she couldn't brush her hair. No wonder – her hands had gone. Beyond her elbows, her arms ended in sausage-like stumps. Even before Lily appeared in the mirror behind her, Tasha knew that she'd been robbed.

Lily ran her gel-nails through her peroxide mane.

"New girl's got them," she said.

But Tasha didn't altogether believe her. Lily's bag was wriggling; something was clearly trying to get out.

In the morning, when Tasha was in her mum's bedroom, helping with her breakfast, Lily texted, *Sleep OK*, as if she knew about barging in on Tasha's dreams.

Tasha's mum sank back in her pillows. "Lily again?" she said.

Tasha shrugged, pushing the phone into her pocket. Her mum hated Lily. She couldn't do anything major to stop their friendship, but she tried. "That girl's dangerous." She'd actually said that, so melodramatic, after she caught Lily rummaging through their bathroom, checking out her pills.

Tasha's mum would never understand about Lily, and there weren't the words to explain – all those crazy, laughing times, and that amazing night when they'd crawled out onto Lily's roof. Lily tickling her to breaking point when she'd tried to count the stars…

Tasha's mum touched her elbow.

"Be careful, love," she said, but she sounded more tired than angry, and her fingers, light as straw these days, were easy to brush off.

Maybe Tasha should have answered Lily's text sooner, or been less eager during History, actually putting up her hand. Throughout the lesson, Lily wouldn't look at Tasha, let alone talk to her, and at the end she slammed her desk into Tasha's, knocking her pencil case to the floor.

Scrambling about for her highlighters and newly-cracked calculator, it took Tasha a moment to register the new girl crouching too.

"Here," she said, passing Tasha her sharpener.

Although the room was stuffy, the girl's gloves were back on. Tasha found herself again admiring their buttons, and that particular green... it didn't seem possible, that monster-hand underneath –

"You ok?" the girl said, her face hovering close.

She was pretty, Tasha realised. The freckles weren't *that* bad, sort of tea-coloured, and her eyes were blue like Lily's – except they weren't like that at all –

In the doorway, Lily was finally looking at Tasha, and no one's gaze could compare to that.

Tasha pulled away from the new girl. "Piss off, freak," she said.

That evening, Lily's texts came thick and fast. Tasha read them, perched on her bedroom windowsill, puffing skunk-clouds into the night.

I heard her step-mother did it with an axe.

Her Granny with a mincing machine –

An accident with her dad's car...

But while Tasha knew what Lily wanted, she couldn't think of anything funny to text back. Instead, she took another drag on the joint. Her Mum was just a wall away, but it wasn't likely she'd get caught. The nurse had left and her mum would be dosed up by now. She probably hadn't made it out of bed all day.

The phone chirped again. *That's where her dead twin was attached.*

Tasha found herself picturing the new girl turning her face away from Lily, as if Lily's eyes had no effect.

She set the phone down. Her fingers were sticky from gripping it, but apart from the tiny, star-shaped mark on her wrist, her hand looked strong and ruddy, flushed with health.

The mark was another reminder of Lily, of a dare gone wrong, but Tasha felt a sudden, jabbing guilt. No one cared about her like Lily. Nobody else understood the urge she felt to blank out sometimes, to blur the edges, or drop into another world completely. All those hours on Lily's roof – all that rolling about, that tickling. They'd woken later with their skinny legs tangled, pressed up close for warmth.

Tasha peered through the dope smoke, searching the darkness, but the sky tonight was thick with clouds. The only star was the one she wore on her arm, from Lily's sizzling cigarette.

During Art, Tasha watched the new girl. The week before, they'd sketched their hands.

Tasha wasn't really into drawing but she'd enjoyed the exercise, studying the bumps and whorls, wondering where the lifeline was, which was the heart?

But there was just a boring still life to paint today, a dusty bottle and some wizened apples, and the new girl had only taken her right glove off. There was something disappointing about those ordinary fingers, clutching her brush.

Still, Tasha was distracted. She spent the lesson mixing paint, trying to find the perfect green.

"You can't take your eyes off her," Lily said. "Is it some perverted lezzer thing?"

"Don't be stupid," Tasha replied. "She's a freak, isn't she? Anyway, you know I don't like girls."

Lily smirked. "Prove it," she said. "I dare you. You can steal her gloves."

It would be easy; the girl couldn't wear her gloves for PE, and Tasha would sneak back to the changing room while the rest of them shivered on the netball court. There was a substitute teacher. She wouldn't be missed, and yet Tasha remained reluctant, and not just because of the mission itself. A part of her wanted to see that hand in action, how it caught and threw.

But Lily bundled Tasha into the toilets, opening her mouth with her fingers before slipping something small and powdery onto her tongue. The pill tasted as synthetic as Lily's nails.

"What is it?" Tasha asked, thinking of the medicine bottles in her bathroom, lined up in their stupid-hopeful rows.

But Lily wouldn't answer. "Swallow," she said.

It didn't take long for Lily's gift to start working. Tasha's echoing footsteps in the empty changing room made her giggle and she could feel her skin rippling. Soft, popping bubbles fizzed from her face to her shoulders and ran down both her arms. Her hands, at the end of them, made her laugh. They bounced through the bleached air like puppet-hands, swaying as if on strings, and as she danced her fingers along the wall tiles, they transformed again, becoming fluttering butterfly-things.

They stopped when Tasha reached the new girl's clothes. Her uniform was heaped on the bench between the other girls' piles, the gloves folded on top. Up close, they were more perfect than ever, gleaming as green as envy, their wrist buttons gazing back.

Tasha lifted them slowly. They felt cool and smooth, nothing like seaweed or avocados – more like how a seal might feel. She held them to her face and their leathery scent was surprisingly sweet. Tasha pictured lush grass and emerald tides. Her fizzing waves grew stronger.

With that electricity shivering through her, Tasha remembered Lily's tickling – and then she was thinking about her mum's hands, the way they used to feel, tugging Tasha close, or stroking her hair. Before her mum got sick, her hands had been so much fuller, weighted and fleshy and warm.

Tasha must have lost track of time, because abruptly the door crashed open and the changing room was filling up with rosy cheeks and smudged mascara, with shouts and shrieks and sweat. Lily pushed through the other girls and stared at Tasha, at the green leather cradled to her chest.

"For fuck's sake," Lily said, "give them here."

But then the new girl appeared beside Lily, and her gaze was just as blue.

"Here," Tasha said, offering her back her gloves.

Lily's eyes grew icy. "What's wrong with you, Tash?" she said. "I knew I couldn't trust you. I always thought you were fucked up…" On and on Lily went, her voice rising, growing shrill and ugly, but it didn't matter. The girl's left hand understood. It reached out, scarred and swollen, its bloated fingers spreading wide.

But it wasn't grabbing for the gloves. Instead, that hand was curling over Tasha's, those freakish fingers brushing hers. Straightaway, Tasha knew that touch, not for its strangeness but its warmth.

Megan Taylor

Unsuitable

THIS IS AN ENDING.

There's a song in the April wind. Its melody is exquisitely sad. The sun is a daffodil-white pool and, when the rain comes, it falls to the soil like blown seeds.

Edward squeezes my left hand. With my right, I pick up my skirts and we run to our secret hideaway. We trip over tree stumps, around fairy rings. Through the fields, where the corn will grow with the summer. Behind the church, through the yew trees which scratch our cheeks, down the stone path through the graveyard – deeper, deeper, into the copse. The clean spring day laps at our backs. I'm numb with laughter and strained with crying.

We hurtle past the forgotten piece of river. Until I pause. It was here that in the winter, Jimmy – the gamekeeper's son – plunged through the ice and was unable to climb out. On the way back from church, they saw him there, gripping a tumbled bough to keep himself afloat. Of course, the branch couldn't protect him from the cold. The audience watched his lips purple and heard the January landscape echo his whimpers, yet nobody detached themselves from the group to crawl across to him. By the time rescue came, he was long dead. My Aunt Adelia came to tell me, a holy look around her mouth. I was in bed with a fever at the time and am ashamedly glad I didn't have to witness the tragedy. I would never rest again if I were plagued with memories of desperate mewls, of a frozen corpse drifting.

"What's wrong?" Edward asks.

I turn away from the hungry water and try to giggle a little more.

At the roots of the willow, we collapse and lie beneath its canopy. Its curls brush against my thighs. My thoughts dissolve as Edward kisses my neck.

"You're beautiful," he says, twisting my hair around his forefinger.

We pretend that the birds aren't quietening and that the day is still a child. He leans into me. I listen for the rustle of feet which are not those of squirrels or muntjacs, but no one ever lingers here. Except for us.

We breathe in time with everything.

The shadows stretch themselves out, until they take up the light that bathes the ground. A chill sidles into the air. When dusk has collected, he escorts me home. He places a kiss on my forehead before he leaves me at the gate. We look at each other.

Goodbye, cries the owl. Goodbye.

I watch him walk away, until he appears to become one of the shadows. He's going to marry Theodora Mannering, a girl whom his parents deem to be Suitable. Perhaps they overlook the fact that I live at the Big House and think I'm *Un*suitable: reckless, inquisitive, peculiar. Most people think me these things. In any case, I don't think Edward's sour-faced mother can bear the thought of her son being happy. He and I are in love, and he isn't in love with awful, prissy Theodora. He swears he isn't. But what can one do, except resign oneself to the truth, and feel hollow?

Tomorrow, I am going to America. I'm to board an allegedly magnificent steamer and be demure at all times as it sails purposefully across the ocean. Miss Mallard, who was my governess when I was younger, will be my companion. She'll find work there. I, for my sins, shall live with my father's sister and her husband, both of whom I've never met, and make my own Suitable Match. I'm never to come back, unless my American society husband makes the trip to work in London and I accompany him. One day.

I daresay I'll have learnt to be another person by then.

Aunt Adelia, who, with my Uncle Ernest, has been my guardian ever since I can remember, sent for me last month to inform me of all this. I feel she has always rather wished that she could ask the maids to stow me away in some cupboard or other. This plan to get rid of me is even more effective. "I'm sorry," I said, choking, my hair escaping its bun, tears running off my jawline. "For whatever it is I've done to make you want to send me away."

She rolled her eyes. I withered. "Do stop being theatrical," she said. "It is not a punishment. It's simply time for your father's family to take their turn, considering all we have done for you. Now go and tidy yourself."

She hasn't spoken to me about it since, regardless of my approaching transatlantic passage being a much-visited topic of conversation amongst her friends. The discussion, however, is usually based around the ship I'll be aboard, and not around my leaving. "My Alfred is *envious*," Mrs Cambridge twittered when she came to tea last week, showing her buck teeth. The other ladies cooed. Aunt Adelia smiled frostily. I attempted to smooth my forehead of the frown that fought to lock my eyebrows together.

As the last of today slips through my fingers, I walk the corridors. I say goodbye to everything. To the hall, where the chandelier glares, the staircase spirals and the grandfather clock stands, his posture avuncular, his pulse constant. To the drawing room, with the velvet curtains, the chatter of evenings gone by turned to dust on the mantelpiece. Although I'll see them in the morning, I say goodbye to the maids individually. I ensure that there's no sign of anyone (especially Aunt Adelia) before hugging Maud. Maud, who ticks me off in a big-sisterly manner when I tear my petticoats, and gossips with me about Edward. She weeps now. As does Cook when I say goodbye to her. She has been good to me. I'm not supposed to eat very many sweets, to avoid growing too stout for my clothes, yet I recently went through an unpleasant phase of feeling nauseous at regular intervals, and a sticky bun or square of shortbread from the kitchen would cheer me considerably when the waves struck. I shall never forget her kindness – or her discretion. Aunt Adelia has never found out about any of the secret snacks.

I wipe my face fiercely with my fist. It aches to go.

In my room, I don't sleep. Instead, I count the stars. I'll be more thorough in my counting when I'm at sea, looking up into acres of black occasionally divided by starry jewels. I'll form my own constellation and leave it in the sky for Edward, so that when he lies awake next to Theodora, he'll think only of me. This is a small comfort. I hold onto it as dawn splits open. My eyelids are finally closing when I'm pulled from my bed to wash, eat breakfast, dress. I hear Dale, the chauffeur, starting the car on the drive.

Maud tugs hard to lace my corset. "Too many buns, I reckon, miss." It should be a comical remark, yet there's something unnerving in her eyes, like a coming storm hovering over the horizon. The anchor of my heart unwinds inside my ribcage. She gulps, squeezes my shoulders and leaves the room, nibbling at her lip.

I don't like lengthy car journeys at the best of times. This one is particularly melancholy. The clouds look as though they have been carded with a hairbrush. Somewhere in an expanse of countryside, an early dragonfly appears, speeding along beside the window. I know she's staring at me. I don't have the nerve to tell her it is rude to stare. In her gossamer fragility, she's formidable.

"Aren't you scared?" I ask her. Her wings shine as if to tell me she's unafraid. She's free. Then she leaves.

I lean my head against the glass.

It's when we arrive that I come to life again. The atmosphere is a tide of its own, catching us, pulling us along. I have heard the murmurs, the stories about this great new steamer. I gaze up at her. The sheer size of her tautens my nerves. I've been told to expect a gigantic ship, yet I hadn't envisaged anything as vast as this until now, with her in front of me. It makes me think of how Maud once said that making love was the most wonderful thing in the world. I assumed I could imagine how the most wonderful thing in the world would be, yet when I first lay with Edward and felt every inch of me glow, I realised I hadn't been close to understanding what she'd meant.

"Here we are," Miss Mallard whispers. She takes my hand. (My little-girl self would have never believed that there would come a morning on which her fierce governess would hold her hand and travel alongside her across the Earth.) We step onto the first-class gangplank. Below, I notice the second-class passengers boarding; the steerage passengers underneath them. The ones who are Unsuitable for the luxurious life we'll have onboard. I watch four steerage children chase one another. Their playful yelps and tiny mouse bodies remind me of little Jimmy from the village – alive, running into the green-red-golden forest with his father throughout last year's autumn months, chortling, oblivious as to what was to come.

Tears turn my vision to smoke. I blink, blink, blink. We move slowly, gracefully, continuing to drink in the ship's enormous proportions. I marvel at the stance of her four funnels; her splendour. The horizon is largely obscured by her, an insignificant line between air and sea. She could be an entire town of her own. She is a phenomenon.

I fizz like the illicit pear drops I used to buy from the village shop. Maybe this could be a beginning. I shall send for Edward when we arrive in New York, give him my new address; tell him to also cross the Atlantic, before the date of his wedding. Then I'll slip out at sunrise and wait for him at the harbour, my hair loose, just like the first night we-

Hush.

There is movement inside me. Where it's supposed to be dark and still.

Hush.

There it is again.

Again.

Again.

Again.

There must be a reasonable explanation. It might be intoxicating grief. Or an odd form of excitement. Or fear. Perhaps it's a sparrow nesting in the pit of my stomach, warming its eggs, waiting for the chicks to hatch at any moment.

Yet of course I know.

I'm not a fool. The sickness. The weight of me. Maud's face this morning. The moon was full when I last had my visitor. I remember thinking how fat it was as I looked at it from my bed, the familiar sensation of deep bruising unfurling in my belly.

How many times has the moon changed since?

My ears thunder. The Earth tilts at its poles. We walk on, dry land retreating through the cracks until it's replaced with the gleaming surface of gloomy depths. The air is too thick for me to breathe. I take it in quickly, shallowly, my head meringue-light, the bulb in my chest twitching. There is nothing. No passengers on gangplanks high or low or in between, in finery or in worn garments. No stewards or ship's officers in uniform. No boat whistles. No Miss Mallard, keeping me steady with her cool hand. No swarms of people, cheering and shouting their farewells. No graceful, proud ship, with her boundless extravagance. Nothing.

Nothing but the flutter in my abdomen, and the gestures of the April light against the water.

Olivia Tuck

All Things Bright and Beautiful

"H AVE YOU EVER seen a hamster before?" asked Anne Marie. She reached a hand inside the cage and with one finger, gently investigated a nest of straw. Emma lowered her head. She thought, "No," but she thought twice, because truth could be tricky – she wanted to look at the question from all angles. To think what the consequences might be.

"Have you?" said Anne Marie. Emma looked at her friend – at Anne Marie's face. An open, happy face, like the sun who'd got his hat on. Or like one of the golden-haired children in the 'Suffer little children…' poster in church. The bottom of the poster said something about the kingdom of heaven belonging to such as these. With her white socks and neat plait, Anne Marie was definitely such as these. The truth was not tricky for her.

"Have you?" she said again. Emma shook her head.

"His name's Goldie," said Anne Marie, folding her fingers around something in the straw. She lifted out the hamster. He was golden-brown and sagged like a beanbag, trimmed at each corner with a tiny pink foot – the smallest Emma had ever seen. His ears were tiny too, and folded and tucked so neatly, they might have been made by fairy hands or God's tidiest angels. He had black-bead eyes. When Emma looked into them, he looked back and there was a sort of dancing spark inside: his own knowing and his own life. This so moved her that the sun seemed to come out all at once, making everything bright and beautiful. Warm, yellow light spread through her – almost all the way.

"They come from Syria," said Anne Marie. Emma thought that Anne Marie sounded young sometimes, though they were the same age. It was because Anne Marie was so sure – a sort of sure that came from not knowing. Like Adam and Eve before the apple. Emma knew too much. And not enough. Enough not to be sure of anything. Syria sounded unlikely: It was a place in the Bible – far away.

"You got him from Syria?" Emma asked, deliberately casually. Anne Marie shook her head – a quick, definite no, which embarrassed Emma. She lowered her brow so that she could peep out from behind her fringe.

"Hamsters. Hamsters come from Syria. But not Goldie," said Anne Marie. "We got him from Mear's Pet Supplies. They do fish – goldfish and stuff. Hamsters too. And rabbits and mice and sawdust and pellets..." The list went on. *So no lie then*, thought Emma – only the truth could come out like that – gushing like water from a tap. She imagined Anne Marie in a confessional. Sins that made God only smile: a confession box full of not coming quick when Mummy called and forgetting to make her bed. She watched her friend's guiltless hands, one cupped for the hamster to sit in, the other fluttering like a butterfly, as Goldie set about clambering up her wrist. Giggling, Anne Marie lifted him back down. The hamster sat blinking at the world, sure of the hand holding him. Emma smiled. Just looking at him, she felt lighter and brighter as if she could un-know, but she couldn't, quite.

"How do you know he's a boy?" she asked. Anne Marie shrugged and sucked the end of her plait.

"They said so at the shop."

"He hasn't got a thingy," Emma thought, but didn't say.

"Do you want to hold him?" said Anne Marie, offering up Goldie as if he were a cupcake. Emma did, but she shrank into herself and shook her head. She feared that somehow, whatever was bright and beautiful in the hamster would know. Her hands would tell.

"Don't be scared," said Anne Marie, gently unloading her little cargo into Emma's hands. Emma felt the barely-there weight of him in her palm, the press of his minuscule paws, and she felt a rush of tenderness. It was as if she'd been whispered a good secret, which made her feel so close to being one of the wise and wonderful that her chest welled and swelled with it. But then Anne Marie said, "I'll get his exercise ball from the kitchen. He might escape, so I'll close the door."

The shadows in Emma's mind lengthened, and the shapes that hid there shifted. She said, "I don't want –" but before she could finish, Anne Marie trotted off, saying, "I'll be right back."

Emma held still, ears and eyes alert: behind closed doors, bad things happened. She didn't know exactly why, but there were reasons. She could feel them – the guilt creeping up from behind, tapping on her shoulder, whispering, "Didn't Mummy tell you not to stand too close to Father Saunders?" She could feel God breathing. He knew. Father Saunders said so: God was all-knowing, all-seeing. If He turned a blind eye, was it because she deserved it?

Standing there, Emma better understood Eve – why she'd wanted Adam to eat the apple too. Emma was fully alone with what she knew. One-of-a-kind alone. Alone as the one true God. And holding the hamster didn't help – he probably didn't even realize she was there. Emma raised a finger and ran it down the semi-circle of Goldie's curved back. Perhaps to him, that was the hand of God? He began making his way up her sleeve and she herded him down to safety, feeling what a terrible thing it is to hold a life. She felt the flutter of his heart, the shell-thin casing of his ribs. She felt the thrill of holding something fragile – not to be the one too small – not to be constrained by someone stronger. Not to be the one suffering God's blind eye – or worse the open eye of one who sees – who enjoys?

She squeezed the hamster, just a little. His feet scrabbled and his head strained. The thread of his spine flexed; it would thrash if it could, but she held it firm. This too Emma knew: to be held by force – but also by a body frozen – knees that will no longer bend or straighten on command, a rib cage that spasms rather than rises and falls; to be constrained by her own skin. Now she controlled two bodies: hers and the hamster's. Emma squeezed more, feeling the hamster's flesh filling out between her fingers. Still, the poor hamster didn't comprehend. Its eyes bulged, dumb and desperate. She wondered how hard she'd have to squeeze till they popped right out.

And she held that thought, feeling good and bad the way it felt good and bad behind the door of the sacristy – only now *she* was the powerful one. She could cause pain or slaughter. She could watch from a great height as another suffered, and feel nothing but satisfaction. Or turn a blind eye. Or feel pity and do good. She could be a good god, like Anne Marie's – like the God of girls who are not invited to confess in the sacristy. The God of all things bright and beautiful. Or she could be God of the Massacre of the Innocents. And she stood poised on that tightrope, feeling the full weight of her power as she quivered this way and that. The hamster stilled. From him came just a sporadic flicker of movement, like the leaps of a dying flame. She could extinguish or save him.

'Save him!' called a quiet voice inside. It was her own; the voice of a girl silently screaming 'help'.

The door handle turned. Anne Marie entered, all happy bluster. In three skips she was at Emma's side, with the exercise ball in hand. Emma looked down and saw that her grip had loosened. In her hands the hamster sat, blinking with astonishment, its silky fur spiked with sweat. Emma stroked the fur smooth. Anne Marie's hand helicoptered in, lifted Goldie, and deposited him in the exercise ball. As Emma watched this benevolent god closing the ball and giving it a little shove, she filled with thanks and hallowed-be-thy-names: she'd been saved – saved from finding out who she was – what she was. Saved from knowing more.

Beaming, Anne Marie asked, "Did you like it?"

Emma thought to lie; she was going to say 'yes' but she felt something bouncing inside, like a sunbeam trying to nudge its way through cloud. She thought twice. She thought to say 'thank you, thank you, thank you,' but bit her lip so as not to let the words slip. She feared the truths that might come streaming out with them. She feared that she might cry.

So she placed herself with one foot in the shadows and one in the light. She shifted head and shoulders in a movement that was nod, shake and shrug, all at once, she looked Anne Marie in the eye, and she said, "It was okay."

PV Wolseley

Notes on Contributors

ZITA ADAMSON is a writer and freelance radio producer based in Bristol. She's had two novels published by Hodder & Stoughton and short stories broadcast on Radio 4. She loves Bach, islands and cloud-watching.

TABITHA BAST has written for *Eclectica Magazine, Plan C, Novara Media, Shift Magazine* and *Dysophia*. She was a contributor to the book *Occupy Everything*, and the *Leeds Riot* zine, which was published in response to Jimmy Cauty's Aftermath Dislocation Principle riot tour. She lives with a child and cat in a cooperative community in inner-city Leeds.

JL BOGENSCHNEIDER has had fiction published in a number of print and online journals, including *Vol. 1 Brooklyn, Necessary Fiction, Passages North, Hobart* and *Ambit.*

DIANNE BOWN-WILSON was born in England, grew up in New Zealand and now lives in Dartmoor. In recent years she's had numerous short stories placed in competitions and included in anthologies. A collection of thirty-two of her successful stories, *Instructions for Living* was published in 2016.

SJ BRADLEY is a writer, editor & organiser from Leeds. She is a Saboteur Award winner for her editing (*Remembering Oluwale,* Valley Press 2016) and a K Blundell Trust Award winner. She has been writer in residence for First Story, and is the director of the Northern Short Story Festival, now in its third year. Her short fiction has appeared in *Litro, Queen Mobs* and *Willesden Herald,* among others, and she is Fiction Editor at *Strix* magazine. Her second novel, *Guest,* is available now from Dead Ink Books.

ANDREA BRITTAN's writing has been coloured by over two decades spent living in Hong Kong. She writes mainly fiction and is currently seeking representation for her first novel, *Owner of a Lonely Heart*. She now lives in rural Derbyshire where she leads workshops for a local writers' group.

SARAH BROOKS works in East Asian Studies at the University of Leeds. She has had stories published in *Interzone*, *Lighthouse* and *Strix*, and is a member of the Leeds Writers' Circle.

EMILY BULLOCK won the Bristol Short Story Prize with her story 'My Girl', which was also broadcast on BBC Radio 4. She has short stories published in other prize anthologies, including *Remembering Oluwale*. She has an MA in Creative Writing from the University of East Anglia and completed her PhD at the Open University, where she also teaches Creative Writing. Her debut novel, *The Longest Fight*, published by Myriad 2015, was shortlisted for the Cross Sports Book Awards, and listed in *The Independent*'s Paperbacks of the Year.

DAVID BUTLER's most recent novel, *City of Dis* (New Island), was shortlisted for the Kerry Group Irish Novel of the Year 2015. His second poetry collection, *All the Barbaric Glass*, was published in 2017 by Doire Press.

VL COWAN was born and raised in Northumberland. She is a legal editor in West Yorkshire, where she is working on a collection of short stories and a longer verse narrative. She will happily make you a cup of tea.

KIM FLEET lives in the Cotswolds with a very bossy cat who helps the creative process by standing on the delete key. Kim enjoys patchwork, making jewellery, and baking, and can often be found writing in coffee shops.

DOMINIC GRACE is a writer from South Leeds. His fiction includes plays, award-winning prose and essays on current affairs. He is currently making a hour-long documentary for Radio 4 on themes of propaganda, class and the problems of patriotism.

SUSAN HODGETTS is a writer and actor with an MA in Writing for Performance. She has had plays produced at the Network Theatre, RADA, and the Theatre Royal, Portsmouth, where she won the Jilted Generation competition. Her short story 'My City' was selected as a City of Stories winner (2017) by Spread the Word and is published in the *City of Stories* Anthology.

MANDY HUGGINS' writing has won numerous awards, and her work has been published in several anthologies and literary journals, as well as in the *Guardian, Telegraph, Reader's Digest, Wanderlust, Mslexia* and *Writers' Forum*. Her first flash fiction collection will be published by Chapeltown Books in 2018.

MAUREEN LENNON is a graduate from the MA at Leeds University in Writing. She is a co-founder of the new writing company Bellow Theatre. Writing credits include three shows for Assemble Fest, as well as *Bare Skin On Briny Waters* (HeadsUp/UK tour 2016/17*), A Long Way Home* (Paines Plough/Hull Truck Theatre 2017) and *A Long Morning Quiet* (The Crucible 2017). She is a West Yorkshire Playhouse FUSE writer.

ELIZABETH OTTOSSON is a writer and translator whose stories have been shortlisted for awards on two continents. In 2016 her flash fiction, 'Grace', won the Segora International Vignette Competition. She is based in Manchester, and is working on a novel.

ANDREY PISSANTCHEV has lived in Leeds for almost exactly ten years, having moved here from Sofia, Bulgaria. He works as a programmer, and is currently an active member of the Leeds Writers and Poets writing group.

MEGAN TAYLOR is the author of three novels, *How We Were Lost*, *The Dawning* and *The Lives of Ghosts*, and a short story collection, *The Woman Under the Ground*. She was chosen as one of TSS Publishing's 'Selected Writers 2017-18' and her stories have appeared, or are forthcoming, in several other publications including the Brighton Prize Anthology 2017.

OLIVIA TUCK has had poetry and pieces of fiction published in a couple of places, and was shortlisted for the 2017 Hysteria Writing Competition. She is due to start at Bath Spa University this year, to study for a BA in Creative Writing.

PV WOLSELEY was born in London in 1976. She graduated from the Courtauld Institute of Art and is studying for a post-graduate degree in creative writing from Manchester Metropolitan University. Her short fiction has been published in Paris Lit Up and Flash Frontier.

'A Delicate Balance', Sarah Brooks
'All Things Bright and Beautiful', PV Wolseley
'The Change', Kim Fleet
'The Final Delivery', Andrea Brittan
'Touched', Megan Taylor
'Wonderland', Maureen Lennon

WINNERS:

1st place: 'A Delicate Balance', Sarah Brooks
2nd place: 'The Final Delivery', Andrea Brittan
3rd place: 'All Things Bright and Beautiful', PV Wolseley